The Slightest Distance

Henry Bromell

The Slightest
Distance

Winner of a Houghton Mifflin
Literary Fellowship Award

HOUGHTON MIFFLIN COMPANY BOSTON 1974

The author is grateful for permission to reprint four lines from
"Mythistorema" by George Seferis from *Collected Poems* 1924-1955,
translated by Edmund Keeley and Philip Sherrard (copyright ©
1967 by Princeton University Press). Reprinted by permission of
Princeton University Press and Jonathan Cape Ltd.

All of the stories in this book, except for "The Girl with the Sun
in Her Eyes," appeared originally in *The New Yorker*. "The Girl
with the Sun in Her Eyes" appeared originally in *The Atlantic*.

FIRST PRINTING W

Library of Congress Cataloging in Publication Data
Bromell, Henry.   The slightest distance.
I. Title.
PZ4.B86814S   [PS3552.T634] 813'.5'4   74-9775
ISBN 0-395-19408-3

Printed in the United States of America

for my mother and father

"We knew that the islands were beautiful
somewhere round about here where we're groping—
a little nearer or a little farther,
the slightest distance."

—George Seferis

Contents

Heart of Light

SAM RICHARDSON sat behind his desk on the second floor of the State Department and thought that, without faith in gravity, he might well ascend through the ceiling into the pale June sky and disappear. The building around him hummed with energy. The flickering fluorescent lights, the computers, the electric typewriters, the water coolers—everything was plugged in. He looked at his watch. Five-thirty. Time to go home. He remembered vaguely his wife's saying something about dinner guests. Who? The Taylors, he thought. He shivered—the air-contioning made the building so cold he wished he'd worn a sweater.

"Good night, Sam."

He looked up and saw his secretary, Sue Benson, standing in the doorway. She held her pocketbook in both hands. "Good night," he said. "Have a good weekend."

"And you get some sleep, Sam," she said, closing the door behind her.

He rose and walked to the window. Through the venetian blinds he could see the parking lot below, the small shapes of fellow bureaucrats walking to their cars. He thought how easy it would be to step out the window and join them.

This feeling of improbable flight had been growing all day. If he wondered for even a second why his desk remained fixed to the floor, why the building itself did not topple, he found himself at the edge of a sensation as bewildering as childhood. The objects in his office, the square efficiency he usually found reassuringly simple, today seemed ugly and unreliable.

He turned from the window and cleared off his desk, then took the elevator to the parking lot and walked to his gray Plymouth. The green plastic seats were hot. He pulled off his jacket and rolled down the windows.

Driving home, he stopped at a red light near C Street. The large plate-glass store windows were slowly turning a dull yellow. On the corner, bottles in hand, some Negroes stared into his car, their wrinkled, puzzled faces glowing. The light changed and he continued through the city, circling the crowded Lincoln Memorial and crossing the bridge to Virginia. The air was warm and heavy. Through the hum of the highway he heard, or sensed, the buzzing of crickets. On his left, the Potomac lapped and sparkled. A few boats were out on the water; their masts cast long, thin shadows toward the shore. Then he was in Alexandria, driving past the small row houses, the willows, the shopping centers, Hot Shoppes, Woodward & Lothrop, the gas stations, the drive-ins.

Sam lived with his wife and three sons in a narrow house in a poor section of Alexandria. His theory was that the wealthier part of town, down by the river, would soon become overcrowded and expand in his direction, eventually subsuming his street. When this happened, the house he had purchased for twenty thousand dollars would be worth forty thousand dollars. *If* this happened. He sometimes suspected—parking the car and stepping out onto the sidewalk—that Prince Street would remain a perpetual euphemism, that the asphalt-brick housefronts would never know improvement.

The brass knocker rapped as he opened and closed the front door. The hallway was cool. He turned to his right and walked through the living room, through the dining room, and into the kitchen. His wife, Laura, was at the sink, rinsing strawberries. Scobie, nine, and Matthew, six, were eating their supper at the counter. They were both dressed in summer pajamas and smelled of soap and baby powder.

"Hello," he said. He kissed Laura on the neck.

"Hello," she said. "How was your day?"

"Too long." He rolled up his shirtsleeves and sat down next to his sons.

"Dad, are we really going away?" Matthew asked, pulling at his red bangs.

"Yes."

"Where?"

"Baghdad."

"Where's that?"

"In the Middle East," Scobie said.

"How will we get there?"

"Fly."

"In an airplane?"

"Yes."

Over his sons' heads, Sam could see the small garden behind the house—the brick flowerbeds and the green tin toolshed and the massive willow tree whose roots threatened to lift one end of the house into the air. He lit a cigarette.

"Dad?"

"Yes."

"How do you get in an airplane?" Matthew asked.

"They lower a ladder," Laura said, turning from the sink. "You climb into the sky." She laughed. "O.K., boys, bedtime."

"Aw, Mom, I'm not tired."

"Bedtime," Sam said.

The boys slipped down off their stools and started for the front stairs.

"Call me when you've brushed your teeth," Laura said.

After they had gone, Sam said, "Hello, love."

"Hello, love." She leaned down and kissed him. "Tired?"

"Yes. Do I have time for a bath?"

"Plenty."

He left the kitchen and climbed the stairs to the bedroom. Quentin, his youngest son, was asleep in his crib. Scobie and Matthew were giggling in the bathroom. Dropping his loose change and car keys on the bureau, Sam slowly undressed, then lay down to wait for the bathroom. He had just lit a cigarette when the telephone rang.

"Hello?"

"Hello? Sam?"

"Hello, Mom." He leaned back and stared up at the graying ceiling. "How are you?"

"I'm fine, dear. How are the kids? And Laura?"

"We're all fine."

"Dear, I wanted to know when you're leaving."

"In six weeks. August third. But we'll be up to see you for a few days before we go. We're flying from New York. How's Dad?"

"He's fine, dear. He sends you his love." She cleared her throat. "We've been having beautiful weather here. The roses are blooming. And we saw Morgan Shaw the other day. Do you remember Morgan? He asked after you."

"Yes, I remember Morgan."

"Have the boys gone to bed?"

"Yes, Mom, I'm afraid they have. I'll tell them you called."

"What does Scobie want for his birthday?"

"That's not for months yet."

She was silent.

"Mom, I've got to get ready for dinner."

"All right, dear. Give my love to Laura."

"I'll call you when our plans are a little clearer," he said.

"Good night, dear."

"Good night."

He replaced the receiver and got up off the bed and walked to the bathroom. Over the sound of running water he could hear his wife, in the third-floor bedroom, reading to Scobie and Matthew. He shut the door and began to shave.

Bob Taylor smiled across the candlelight and said, "Hell, Sam, you just work too hard."

"What Bob means," Jenny Taylor said, "is that *men* work too hard."

Sam looked down at his hands, at his grandfather's gold signet ring twinkling on his little finger. "We work because we aren't supposed to be children anymore," he said.

"Why, Sam!" Jenny exclaimed. "What a charming idea. Does that mean you're a child at heart?"

"Perhaps."

"You wish you didn't have to work?"

"No. I like to work."

Laura cleared the table and carried in four blue bowls of strawberries and brandy.

"What shall we do for the children's birthday this year?" Jenny asked. Alice Taylor, Sam remembered, had been born four hours after Scobie.

"Take them to the zoo," Laura said.

"Or the circus," Bob said.

"I want Scobie to marry Alice," Jenny said, touching Laura's hand and laughing. "I want you to be my sister."

Sam's gaze wandered to the Greek dishes hanging on the wall behind his wife's head: small brown fish swimming in a sea of white. He took off his glasses and rubbed his eyes. The voices of his wife and the Taylors, submerged in darkness, seemed as soothing as the silver and china on the table, the paintings on the wall, the feel of the floorboards under his feet. He opened his eyes and replaced his glasses. The three figures quivered into focus. "Yes," he said, picking up the echo of a remark. "Six weeks."

"Then you won't *be* here for the children's birthday," Jenny said.

"No, I guess we won't. I hadn't thought of that."

"Are you looking forward to going?" she asked.

"Yes."

"I don't want to go anywhere," she said. "I want to stay right here in my little house in Alexandria."

"Oh, come on, Jenny," Laura said. "Wouldn't you like to go to London—or Paris?"

"No. Anyway, the kids would hate to leave their friends."

"Kids adjust," Sam said. "Much better, probably, than we do." As he spoke, it occurred to him that perhaps children objected to being unsettled even more than adults.

Reading his mind, his wife said, "Sometimes."

"I think our children may grow up to be quite insecure," Jenny said. "Traveling so much."

"I wonder if they'll grow up wanting a home," Laura said. "All the things we don't really have. Maybe they'll be very domestic and rooted."

"I wouldn't be surprised," Sam said, pushing back his chair.

He led the way to the living room. Laura brought coffee in on an oval silver tray.

"Laura, wouldn't it be wonderful if Scobie *did* marry Alice?" Jenny clapped her hands and leaned back in her chair and laughed.

After the Taylors had left, after he and Laura had stood

on the front steps and waved goodbye into the purple summer night, Sam went from room to room turning off lights and locking doors. The ashtrays and empty glasses on the table made him nostalgic, as if he had had a good time. Upstairs, he undressed and washed, then slipped into bed beside Laura. She was reading. He took off his glasses and laid them on the floor.

"What's wrong, honey?" she asked.

"I don't know."

"Depressed?"

"A little."

Through the open window he could hear a radio. The words of the song were unintelligible, but the music was fairly clear—a steady beat, a quavering sigh.

"I wonder where we'll be in ten years," Laura asked, turning a page in her book.

"Did you check the boys?" he asked.

She nodded.

"Goddam humid," the fat man in the hardware store said.

It was Saturday afternoon and Sam still had a slight hangover.

Cohen, who owned the store, was slowly wrapping a package of nails.

"God*dam* humid," the fat man said again.

He paid, picked up his package, and with a final, sunburned, neck-wrinkling grin, left the store.

Cohen turned to Sam. "What can I do you for?"

"Just these," Sam said, pointing to a pile of screws on the counter.

"Dad, can we have some pennies?" Scobie asked. He

and Matthew were standing in front of the bubble-gum machine.

"And some pennies," Sam said.

The boys took their pennies and dropped them into the slot, pulled the silver lever, and waited with cupped hands to catch the balls of bubble gum before they hit the floor.

"What kind did you get?" Matthew asked as they left the store.

"Red and yellow."

"I'll trade you a black for a yellow."

"I *hate* black."

The back door of Cohen's opened onto a parking lot. Sam and the boys crossed the blistering tar to Patrick Street, then walked to the alley that ran down the middle of the block behind their house. At the far end of the alley, three men were unloading a delivery van. They moved slowly, stopping every few seconds to wipe their foreheads and puff on their cigarettes.

"There's a ghost in there," Matthew said. He pointed to a deserted wooden house on one side of the alley.

"There's no such thing," Scobie said.

"Larry said there's a ghost in there."

"Larry doesn't know anything," Scobie said. "There's no such thing as ghosts."

Sam opened the back gate and the three of them walked into the garden.

Laura was sitting on one of the low brick walls that circled the flower beds. A scarf was tied around her head and she held a trowel in her hand. Before her, in his crib, Quentin slapped at shadows.

"Mom, when can we go swimming?" Scobie asked.

"Tomorrow. The Taylors have invited us."

"When am I going to learn how to swim?" Matthew asked.

"This summer, if you want."

"I'm going to teach you," Scobie said.

"You can't teach me."

"I can, too. Dad said I could. Didn't you, Dad? Dad said I was as good a swimmer as him." Scobie suddenly stooped and picked at the dirt between the bricks of the garden floor. He stood with a marble in his hand. "A cat's-eye," he said.

"Can I have it?" Matthew asked, straining to see into his brother's palm.

"No. I found it."

"You have to find one of your own," Laura said.

Matthew stared up at the sky. "Where?"

"In the alley," Scobie said.

Matthew swiveled and ran toward the gate. "In the alley!" he cried.

"Don't go far," Laura called.

Scobie slammed the gate behind them.

Sam leaned forward and stroked Quentin's small fingers, then straightened and said, "I'm going to build a flower-bed around the base of the fountain."

"Have you finished the pump?"

"More or less."

The sunlight dropping through the leaves of the willow tree warmed the back of Sam's neck. He looked at Laura, her scarf, the dirt on her fingers. "I've been thinking," he said.

"Yes?"

"You're beautiful."

She blushed. "Thank you."

Sam stared at the wall where he was building his fountain—the small hole for the pump he had drilled that morning. By his feet were a pile of bricks, a bag of cement, and a wheelbarrow full of sand and some gravel. He filled a bucket with water from the garden hose and started mixing the concrete.

"I think I'll take Quentin inside," Laura said, smiling down at the crib. She picked the baby up and walked into the shadows of the house.

As he set the first row of bricks, Sam wondered what his sons would be like when they grew up. He would probably never know; they would grow into themselves, self-contained secrets, and he would spend the rest of his life thinking he had understood them best when they were children.

He stood to ease the pain in his knee.

The light in the garden reminded him of his own childhood. The soft, faded sunshine, the coolness of the leaves and plants, the dry smell of brick—within this garden he sensed an almost religious privacy, a vision of things similar to a child's. Being young was like being rich; promise of perfection was the rule, not the exception. The garden, with its delicately mottled light, was a kind of dream world. His own childhood had been so peaceful, so oblivious to failure, that growing up had become a passage through various levels of cynicism.

"Dad!" The gate slammed open and Scobie and Matthew came running into the garden. They were both crying.

"What's the matter?" Sam laid down his trowel.

"Pig took my forks," Matthew said.

"Your what?"

"Forks," Scobie said. "We found some forks in the alley but Pig took them."

"*Gold* forks." Matthew was sobbing.

"Who's Pig?" Sam asked.

"This big guy who always beats us up. He beats everybody up. He even beat Larry up."

"Dad, they were my forks," Matthew cried. "I found them."

"Come here," Sam said.

He touched Matthew's face. "Do you really care if this character Pig took your forks?"

"I *found* them, Dad."

"I know, but are they really that important?"

"Dad, why would Pig take them?" Scobie asked.

"I don't know. Maybe he doesn't have anything of his own."

"I would have given him a fork."

"I know that. But he doesn't." Sam paused. "Why do you call him Pig, anyway?"

Scobie shrugged. "Everybody calls him that," he said.

"What's his real name?"

"I don't know."

"Do you think that's a nice name to call him—Pig?"

"Dad, he's a *bully*."

"Would you like to be called Pig?"

"No."

"Maybe he wouldn't beat everybody up if they didn't call him Pig."

"He'd beat us up no matter what we did," Scobie said.

"That's right," Matthew said, nodding.

Though their faces were still red and streaked, they had both stopped crying.

"Hey, Dad, when are we going to Nana's?" Scobie asked.

"In a few weeks. Before we leave."

"She has a beach."

"That's right."

"I'm going to learn how to swim," Matthew said.

"I'm going to teach him," Scobie said.

"Dad, I'm hot," Matthew said.

"Why don't you play inside for a while?"

"What can we play?" Scobie asked.

"Cowboys and Indians," Matthew said.

"I'm sick of cowboys and Indians," Scobie said. "Let's play spaceship."

"What's that?" Matthew asked.

"I learned it at school. You know what a spaceship is, Dad?"

"I think so. Why don't you go inside and explain it to Matthew?"

"O.K. Come on, Matthew."

Scobie leading, the two boys crossed the garden and hurried into the house.

Sam wedged a brick down into the mortar, tapped it with the handle of his trowel, and carefully scraped and flicked away the curling lip of excess concrete.

What made bullies? Boys usually fought because they wanted to be men, but what caused indiscriminate hatred? He didn't know. He worried that his sons would not be prepared for it, that, because of his fountains and their mother's fairy tales, they would live by their senses, bruised and saddened. Bringing up children well was not necessarily the same thing as preparing them for life. Scobie and Matthew and Quentin would have to learn to understand power—what it was, how it was used. They would have to learn to understand that Pig was not simply bad but powerful.

From the depths of the house came the sound of the telephone ringing for the fourth time.

Brushing his hands, Sam walked through the cool, green kitchen and into the equally cool but paler dining room. He felt, stepping so suddenly from sun to shadow, as if he were moving in slow motion, a lazy fish in a blue-green aquarium. He was halfway through the dining room when the telephone stopped ringing. He could hear the ship's clock ticking on the mantelpiece, caught a glimpse of chrome sparkling through the front window.

"Ready, X–42?" Scobie called from the hallway.

Sam stopped and listened.

"Ready!" Matthew called down from the third-floor bedroom.

"Control!" Scobie cried. "I'm *Control!*"

"Ready, Control."

"O.K. Countdown. Five, four, three, two, one . . . *Blast-off!*" Scobie growled a high-pitched imitation of a rocket engine.

Matthew said nothing.

"X–42?"

"What?"

"Can you read me?"

"What?"

"What do you see?"

There was a long silence on the third floor.

"X–42? Matthew?"

"What?"

"Tell me what you see. You're in outer space. What do you see?"

There was another long silence, and then Matthew shouted down, exuberant, giddy, "Cowboys and Indians!"

After dinner Scobie and Matthew went upstairs to get into bed, and Sam sat with Laura in the kitchen drinking coffee. The back door was open and he could see long shadows on the brick pathway. A cool breeze floated into the house.

"Did the boys tell you what happened today?" she asked.

"With Pig? Yes. I told them not to call him Pig. That was all I could think to say." He watched her stand and move to the sink, where she started washing dishes.

"Go kiss the boys good night," she whispered. "They're waiting."

He walked through the quiet, dark house and up the stairs, pausing for a moment by an open window and staring out at the alley behind the garden, the parking lot and hardware store beyond. The sounds of the city carried clearly across the deepening dusk: buses, cars, police whistles, sirens, screeching brakes, children's cries. He felt the warmth of the house behind him and turned to climb the stairs to the third floor. Below, his wife switched on the record player.

The room was almost dark.

"Hi, Dad," Scobie said.

"Hi." Sam sat down on the edge of Scobie's bed.

"Hey, Dad, I'm going to learn how to swim," Matthew said.

"I know."

"Dad?"

"Yes?"

"When's Quentin going to start talking?"

"He talks now."

"All he can say is 'No.' "

"Give him time."

"Hey, Dad, guess what?"

"What?"

"That's what!"

They both shrieked with laughter, flapping their sheets.

"Go to sleep," he said softly. He pulled Scobie's sheet up to his chin and kissed him on the cheek.

"Dad?"

"What?"

"Were you ever beat up when you were little?"

"A couple of times. Sure."

"What did you do?"

"Nothing much I could do. Don't worry about it. Go to sleep. Don't forget, we're going swimming tomorrow."

He looked at the two glasses of water on the table between the beds, the stuffed animals, the books and soldiers. He felt as if he had once slept in this room—he could imagine its immensity. What, he wondered, kept it all together? What magic was it that kept this house, the family, from springing apart, disappearing? Again, he felt that, with a swoop of his arms, he might flutter up to the stars and fly away. He crossed to Matthew's bed, untangled his sheets from his legs, and tucked him in. As he leaned down to kiss him, his hand touched something hard. He looked closer. There, clenched in Matthew's curled fingers, was a marble—a cat's-eye. I know nothing, Sam thought, suddenly straightening and staring about the room. Nothing.

He turned and walked downstairs to Laura.

Mime

W HEN, LATER THAT EVENING, some boys ignited their own firecrackers and the sizzling fuses exploded above the grass like small stars, Ken was reminded of the stars swirling in the pattern of Nancy's skirt as she crossed the lawn toward the car.

"Where have you been?"

"Driving," he said, slamming the Falcon door shut.

"I can see that. Where?"

"I took Mom out."

"Oh." His wife looked past his shoulder. "How is she?"

"Better."

They walked together into the house. He could hear his two children playing upstairs. On the wall directly facing the front door hung a framed etching of an eighteenth-century man-of-war. Ken hunched his shoulders as he went down the hallway and into the den, where pain rose up, fast as fear, and pushed him onto the green leather couch. He closed his eyes and listened to the shrill humming in his ears. At the other end of the house, Nancy yanked dinner out of the refrigerator. He heard the sucking thump of the closing door, Keith, his son, screaming, "I did *too*," and, near his head, the steady ticking of a ship's clock.

"Ken!" Nancy shouted. "The grill!"

He opened his eyes and saw his mother's face squinting at him from the wall, gleaming behind glass. Her cheeks were red with rouge, her lips bright red, her suit—the one he would see her in forever—red wool. On her feet she wore sneakers, as if ready to prance, like one of her birds, at the feet of his father.

Sitting up and reaching into his back pocket, Ken pulled out a sheet of yellow legal-pad paper, unfolded it, and smoothed it out on the glass-topped coffee table. It was a letter, written in the precise, back-slanting hand of his older brother:

June 27, 1962

Dear Ken,

I have talked with some friends in the hiring-firing department, and they assure me that, barring unexpected catastrophe on the exams, you could expect to get a job. Thirty-three is not too old to start, though most first-year officers are younger. If you are still interested, write to John Hanley, State Department, Washington, D.C., and he will send you application forms, etc. I can write you a recommendation, if you wish, but I really don't think there will be any problems.

Jordan is hot, but not too humid, so we are struggling along. Laura has started learning Arabic and is doing quite well. Quentin was involved in a minor scandal last week, in that he and his best friend were caught filching loose change to buy candy at the local store. Matthew is getting ready to join Scobie at Eaglebrook this fall and is very excited. He's already packed.

Thanks again for watching over Scobie. I know he's happier staying with you than Mom and Dad. He feels more in contact with the real world, I think. He wrote that you all drove into the city to see *Psycho* and that Nancy got so scared she kicked the person in the seat in front of her!

I haven't been doing much this summer. A few bad watercolors, that's all.

My love to Nancy and the kids. Let me know what you decide about the job.

Love,
Sam

He refolded the letter and rose from the couch.

Narrow French doors led from the den out onto a patio. Lawn lapped at the brick, rolled back to an artificial pond, and broke at a row of hedges. Ken poured charcoal into the grill and doused the flaky black chunks with lighting fluid. He lit a match and the flame snapped upward, hissed, and settled.

For eleven years he had worked in his father's real-estate office. He was still there, emptying his pipes into the same glass ashtrays, staring at the same prints of poised golden retrievers and scattering ducks on the same walls. The pain in his back, the humming in his ears—these were the accoutrements, he felt, of failure. Body and soul—he banged the dimming coals—erode together. Once, long ago, he had almost escaped, but the moment had merely been a brief excitement, an overheard conversation—a hushed, fluttering conversation that had moved in circles as abstract as words. Connections continued to evade him this way. Who was he, this idiot flipping hamburgers on a grill? He could not even recognize his own hands. The thick fingers had bent, or stretched. Sometimes—now, with the keen between his ears—he thought he was someone else.

The lawn was a soft, summer blue. The sky met the field behind the hedges, the invisible suburbs, and burned off the last, pure squares of sunlight. Crickets had started buzzing, and from some neighbor's yard came the squeals and yelps of children and dogs at play.

"Here's a drink," Nancy said, walking through the French doors and handing him a martini. "You look like you need it."

"It's the goddam humming," he said. "It never stops. Where's Scobie?"

"Upstairs. Reading." She peered nearsightedly into the embers. "How're the hamburgers?"

"A few more seconds."

"Oh, by the way, I found the credit cards. They were mixed up with the kids' bathing suits. All wet and sticky. They must have fallen there on our way back from the beach yesterday."

"I got a letter from Sam."

"And?"

"He thinks I can get the job."

"Oh, Ken, really?"

"That's what he said." Ken turned the hamburgers over. "I'd have to pass the exams."

"You could do that."

"Maybe."

"Of course you could."

"Call the mob. Chow time."

She went back into the house and shouted up the stairs, "Keith, Barbara, Scobie! Dinner!"

Selling houses, Ken thought, dropping the hamburgers onto paper plates, was a little like selling advice. He gave people what they thought they needed. Bigger houses, bigger lawns, bigger driveways. He made a living on a bad joke that everyone else thought was funny. Yet here and there he found compensation: small objects discovered in attics and garages—an abandoned Model T, a dusty Victrola, a dirty Tiffany clock—that pleased him with their age, their texture, their unfailing ability, when coaxed, to cough back into life. Occasionally there was even the pleasure of simply selling someone shelter and seeing that shelter reshaping itself into a collage of pennants on bedroom walls, deep carpets on living-room floors, faucets that leaked, blocks on kitchen tables. He saw in his own house, in the myriad adjustments the old frame had made to his family, a similar image—only torn, ripped across the center by impatience.

"Shut *up*, goddammit! Wait a minute."

He pushed back Keith's groping fingers and handed him a plate. Barbara was crying. He passed her a plate. She dropped it on the patio. Keith laughed.

"I said shut up." Ken put another hamburger on Barbara's plate. "Keith, leave her alone."

"Another drink?" Nancy asked from the door.

"Yes."

"Daddy, when are we going to the fireworks?"

"The what?"

"You promised," Nancy called.

"It's the Fourth of July," Keith said.

"That's right." Nancy reappeared and gave him his drink. "Independence Day."

"Oh, Nancy, goddammit, I'm tired."

"You promised."

Her mouth, exaggerating promise, for a second seemed to collapse, toothless, gumless, onto her chin. She smiled, sipped her drink, and sat down on one of the aluminum-and-plastic patio chairs. He stared at her, the sounds and tastes and smells of their courtship whirling together into one fantastic yearning and then vanishing out over the lawn. She crossed her thin, knock-kneed legs and touched her small fingers to her throat.

"What did Dr. Bradshaw say?" she asked, tipping her head back in his direction.

"That it'll probably never go away."

"You'll hear *humming* in your ears the rest of your life?"

"Yeah."

"Hi, Ken."

It was Scobie, standing in the doorway.

"Hi. Grab yourself a hamburger. You've got to be fast if you want anything around here."

Scobie's face was narrow, his brown hair was neatly combed, and his eyes were green, detached and dreamy. He was fourteen. Unlike his father, he cared nothing about the way things—cars, boats, plumbing—worked, and so Ken never knew how to talk to him.

"I got a letter from your father today."

"How is he?" Scobie asked.

"O.K. He says your mother's learning Arabic."

"Ken, did Dr. Bradshaw give you anything to take?" Nancy asked.

"Pills."

"What kind of pills?"

"Pills, for Chrissake, *pills*. How should I know what kind they are? Keith, *leave her alone*. Hamburger?"

"No thanks," Nancy said, shaking her head. "I'm not hungry."

"You've got to eat. You weigh less now than you did ten years ago."

"No, I don't."

"You look it."

"Well, I don't."

Ken walked into the den and made two more martinis. Ten years ago, he had been in Spain with Nancy on their honeymoon, and now, catching in the glinting vodka bottle a flash of those Spanish nights, he hesitated above the glasses and ice and wished for a moment that he could begin again. He remembered walking with Nancy across her New England campus, driving home in his first Pontiac to announce their engagement, sailing on the Sound that first summer after they were married, repairing this house, making the pond he could see through the French doors. These little events should have added up to happiness. But they didn't. Not tonight. Perhaps because whenever he traveled the ten miles to his parents' house and entered once again that cloying atmosphere he returned depressed. He felt stranded, left behind by his brother; a

fantasy he thought they both had shared, a fantasy somehow rooted in Long Island, had turned out to be his alone,
meaningless yet, even now, real: a fantasy of snow and
burning leaves and varnished boats, a fantasy of an old
order that had somehow enabled his family to make one
generation seem like twelve, and its demise the end of an
entire civilization.

Outside on the patio, he sat down next to Nancy and lit
a pipe.

"You feel all right?" she asked.

"Sure. Great. Wonderful."

"Barbara, there are more potato chips in the kitchen."

"I'm getting pretty tired of eating lunch with Dad every
day," Ken said.

"You don't eat with him every day."

"Seems like it."

"It's a nice thing to do."

"It's just getting to be a pain in the ass, that's all."

"It's time to go to the fireworks," Keith said.

"I just got home."

"Daddy, we'll be *late*."

"We should go," Nancy said.

"All right, all right, goddammit!" he shouted. "Carry
your plates in."

Shouting, he felt twice his size, a monster in a doll's
house. Barbara ran for her sweater, Keith kicked open the
screen door, Nancy riffled through her purse for her lipstick. The grass and pond caught the sun's muted colors
and reflected back a mottled sheen. Ken, watching, felt
that the landscape had been stripped of substance, bounc-

ing back—like mirrors in a madhouse—his own image, distorted, mercurial, infinitely pliable. Anger raged with his pain; from nowhere came a desire to shatter, to smash his huge hand down on the small house and obliterate everything it held: woman, children, plates, grill.

"Ken! We're ready!"

"O.K., O.K."

He left the patio and walked into the hallway. Nancy was waiting for him by the front door. She had a red scarf tied around her head.

"Where're the kids?" he asked.

"In the car."

"Daddy!" Barbara screamed out the back window. "We need a blanket!"

"Oh, for Chrissake."

"I'll get it," Nancy said.

His feet crunched over the gravel driveway. He got in behind the wheel of the Falcon. Keith and Barbara were fighting in the back seat. Scobie was trying to keep them apart. Ken leaned over and slapped Keith. Immediately, the boy started crying, his round, suntanned face convulsed into a mask.

"All right, cut it out, both of you," Ken said. "Keith, stop sniveling."

Nancy opened the door and slid in next to him, throwing the blanket onto the seat. "What's wrong with him?" she asked, nodding toward Keith.

"Mean Daddy hit him."

"You shouldn't be so violent."

He raced the car into reverse, spun it around, and sped

out of the driveway. On the road, he drove fast, passing the large brick houses, the cautious lawns, the pretentious gateposts, the bright summer trees. Nancy muttered, "You don't have to drive like a maniac." He pressed his foot down on the accelerator. Reflections spun across the windshield. The humming in his ears and the humming of the car's engine merged, but then, trying to separate the two, he suddenly heard, springing from a silence as tense as an echo deep within his skull, his mother's voice calling him to dinner, and he let himself float down into himself, down into the secret spaces of his heart, where, like a rider on a magic amulet, he saw rising up before him his mother's face—her face twenty years ago, a young face that seemed a memory of a memory—and he realized that this face, this expression, was all that had ever stood between him and freedom. The fantasy of an old order was her fantasy. It was she who made him feel like an ancient prince wandering the paved fields of Long Island. Sam had, by leaving home, made this fantasy a memory, softened and personalized by distance. But Ken lived in it, as though it were a country.

"Well, what do you think?" Nancy asked.

"About what?"

"Sam's letter."

"What about it?"

"Oh, come on, Ken, don't be so snappy."

"I'm sorry. I don't know."

"We'll never leave." Nancy sighed. She stared out the window. "Will we?" she asked, turning and looking at him.

"I don't know."

When he was born, he decided, steering the car into town, he must have fallen from the hospital bed, because for as long as he could remember he had felt he lived in a falling dream, a dream he had actually had many times as a child. This amateurish tapestry—his job, his car, his house, his family—was part of the same dream, the same motion sickness. He was never at rest. He was always just waking up or falling asleep, always on the rim of consciousness, always dreaming that, awake or asleep, he was dreaming. When he was ten, he had discovered in Sam's careful paintings an exotic and remote reasonableness that he had later tried to emulate in perfect, working reproductions of boats and planes. But his efforts had always failed. Not because the models were bad but because, despite their still beauty, his life continued to careen through the falling dream. And whatever he did to destroy the dream was only subsumed by it. The patch of Long Island where he had grown up was now, inevitably, his home. This town was the same town he had once, as a boy, entered with awe. Billy's Barber Shop and the Rialto Theatre and Schumann's Hardware Store, his old dentist's office, his junior high school, the drugstore with a marble-and-brass soda fountain, last year's Christmas wreaths drooping from the telephone poles, the yellow clapboard town museum, the gray, stone, cold Congregational church—they all flicked past the Falcon window like photographs in a family album, distant relatives who had once meant a great deal to him but who now had withered and faded so much that, seeing their faces, he could only feel an indifferent, terrifying sadness.

"Ken, if you get any closer you won't be able to park."

Abruptly, he swung the car into the First National Bank parking lot and turned off the motor. Keith and Barbara, followed by an awkward Scobie, leaped from the back seat. Nancy took the blanket and Ken locked the car.

On Pleasant Street, they followed the crowd toward the high-school football field. A man in front of Ken was carrying his child on his shoulders. The intersection was blocked with cars. Overhead the sky was violet, dissolving to a thin strip of bright orange at the horizon.

The field appeared through the trees, a stretch of green and yellow surrounded by the town's oldest houses. The children, released, jumped into the air and shouted. There was a hot-dog stand set up near the bleachers, around which high-school kids in windbreakers and blue jeans meandered like ghosts. Ken chose a spot near the fifty-yard line and sat his family down on the blanket. Behind him, the bleachers, shifting with children, reached to the sky. As the crowd milled and shuffled and the shadows of telephone poles and trees slid across the football field, some boys ignited their own sputtering fireworks. In the middle of the field, men in baseball caps prepared the Roman candles and flares.

"Daddy, when are we going to see the fireworks?" Keith asked.

"Hold your horses."

Directly in front of the bleachers was a microphone. As the sun balanced on the skyline, as real darkness seemed imminent, a short, bald man walked to the microphone and asked for everyone's attention. He introduced himself: Mayor Sullivan. There was spasmodic applause from the bleachers.

"Thank you." The mayor grinned. "Thank you very much."

He was overweight and nervous, his suit too small, a piece of paper shaking in his hands. He began reading, his words battered and nearly obliterated by a breeze shrieking through the microphone: "We come here together to celebrate the winning of America's independence. Because of that battle we are now a free people. We are happier and richer than any other country in the world. We lead better lives. But freedom is not an easy commodity to keep. We must reflect tonight, I think, on the good fortune we have known and the work that lies ahead if our children are to inherit the same good fortune."

He paused, confused, fumbling with his paper, and stood back from the microphone, his hoarse "Thank you" coming through in a whispery, high-pitched screech.

There was a strong current of applause in the bleachers this time, and the mayor, turning to the field, waved his hand in some kind of signal. Out on the field the men in baseball caps stepped toward the stacks of rockets. The crowd grew quiet, hushed as the evening locked itself into the motion of the mayor's dropping hand. Even Ken held his breath as he waited for the final gesture, the sky itself to black out, before gasping as the first rocket shot into the darkness and exploded above his head in a spinning frenzy of red, white, blue.

The Girl with the
Sun in Her Eyes

THEY WERE LEFT together, staring at each other. She was older, shorter, tending toward heaviness, very blond. Over her shining green eyes the thick black lines that deepened her face suddenly narrowed as she smiled, and he saw the gold circles hanging from her ears, the almost haughty tilt of her head. They were both holding drinks in their hands, standing in a corner of the ambassador's living room, listening to the musical voices around them and watching the tactful Pakistani servants slide among the chatting couples. They were the youngest people at the party. She looked twenty, maybe twenty-one. He saw his father at the other end of the living room talking to a bald Kuwaiti, then looked back at her. In profile, her face was delicate, with a small, upturned nose and a high, wide forehead. She had one arm folded across her breasts. She glanced at him, saw him staring, and stared back, just as the Saudi Arabian consul sorrowfully bowed away and left them alone.

"Hello," she said.

"Hello."

"Who are you?"

"Scobie."

"Scobie who?"

"Richardson."

"Ah." She smiled. "Quentin's big brother."

"That's right. How do you know that?"

"I'm his girl friend's governess," she said. "I live right down the street from you."

Scobie saw his mother sitting on a couch, talking to the ambassador's wife. She held a drink in one hand, on her lap, and a cigarette in the other, her elbow resting on the arm of the couch.

"Who are you?" he asked.

"Mona Brompton."

"And you're English, right?"

"Very," she said, trilling. *"Verrry."*

They both laughed. Her short, strong fingers gripped her glass. She was wearing a long black dress, and a rust-colored shawl covered her shoulders.

"Mona, are you having a good time at this party?"

"In a way, yes." She glanced around the room. "Because it's Christmas, and I can't help enjoying Christmas parties. But in a way, no, because I don't know anyone here. I don't know anyone in the *whole of Kuwait,* as a matter of fact. But that's another story. You're in school in England, aren't you? Quentin told me."

"Yes," he said.

"Do you like it?"

"No. In fact, I may get thrown out."

"Really? Whatever for?"

"Stealing library books."

"Did you steal library books?"

"Yes."

"But why?"

"I don't know."

She laughed, took a sip from her drink, and looked at his stomach, his knees, his face.

"I'm tired," she said, lowering her glass. "Let's sit somewhere."

"Where?"

"Anywhere. Over there." She waved toward an empty loveseat in the corner. "O.K.?"

"Sure."

They sat down together, their legs touching, and lit cigarettes.

"How long have you been in Kuwait?" he asked her.

"Eighteen months, twelve days, six hours and forty-five minutes. Approximately."

"And who do you work for?"

"The Marshes."

"Right. And how many kids do they have?"

"Four."

"And one of them's my brother's girl friend?"

"Kathy."

"Amazing. Tell me more."

"Quentin's been telling me all about you, actually. He's been very excited. He told me you have long hair and that you drink a great deal."

"He did?"

"Yes."

"He told you that?"

"Absolutely."

"Let's go outside," Scobie said.

They left the loveseat and stood on the terrace. There was a full moon, and its pale light rippled over the small waves of the Persian Gulf. The beach looked like a photograph of the moon itself, and there was a slow breeze in the air. They sat down on the wall of the terrace and looked at the shimmering water.

"It never gets cold here," she said.

"What's it like in summer?"

"Hot. One can't move. One just sits inside all day, breathing through one's air-conditioner."

"Weird."

"It is weird," she said. "Very weird. I don't know what I'm doing here."

"Making a living."

"I know. But why *here?*"

"Why?"

"I thought it would be romantic," she said, smiling brightly. "I thought I would be swept away by a handsome billionaire oil sheik."

"Well, I've only been here seventy-two hours or whatever it is, but I can tell you one thing, this place is weird. All those pink and yellow houses. And no trees. Not one tree. And nobody drinks, and nobody smokes."

"Honey?" It was his mother, standing at the open terrace door. "Time for us to go home."

"O.K. I'll be right there."

He wanted to kiss Mona, but felt that it would somehow be obscene—she was so womanly. He sat there for a few more seconds, looking at her, and the sea, then rose and said good night. She grabbed his hand and pulled herself up.

"I'll probably see you around tomorrow," he said.

"Most likely," she said.

Scobie poked his head into the kitchen and said good morning to Hassan. Hassan looked up from the counter, where he was kneading dough, and smiled, baring three gold teeth. Scobie asked for coffee and went back into the living room, put "Rubber Soul" on his parents' Grundig, and sat down at the dinner table. Hassan brought his coffee in and handed him a note from his mother. "Dearest— Don't spend all day in bed. I'll be home for lunch. Isn't Mona pretty? Your mother." He folded the note and lit a cigarette and listened to the Beatles.

After a second cup of coffee he walked to the beach. It was a mild, clear day, and the air smelled like spring. He couldn't believe Christmas was only a week away. He passed by a row of stone houses and through the embassy gates, then down a path to the beach. The gulf was glittering, like a bowl of glass. Two small children were playing in the shallows. Ten feet up the beach, in the shade of a straw fisherman's hut, sat Mona. She saw him and waved.

"Good morning," she said, squinting at him as he bent down into the shadow. She was wearing a scarf and balancing a paperback copy of *Balthazar* on her knees.

Scobie sat next to her on the sand. He could hear the pebbles crinkling in the surf.

"Those two of your wards?" he asked, pointing at the children.

"Yes. The youngest. Benji and Simon. They're quite lovely, actually. I wish the others were so good."

"What are they like?"

"The others?"

"Yes."

"Spoiled brats," she said. "They eat too much. Just like their mum and dad."

"Is Quentin's girl friend, Kathy—is she nice?"

"Not really."

"Then why does he like her?"

"Because she already has breasts." Mona giggled.

Scobie lit a cigarette and lay back with his face in the sun. Mona flipped over a page of her book. The sand was warm under his fingers. He rolled over and looked at the brilliant sea.

"Do you really not know anyone here?" he asked.

"Oh, I know a few people. Friends of the Marshes."

"Don't you ever go out?"

"Once in a while," she said.

"With whom?"

"Oh, just different people. Last week I went out with a prince. He's in exile from Iraq, I think. Anyway, he tried to seduce me. I repulsed him, however. And once I went out with a disgusting businessman who already had sixteen wives, including two Belgians, an Australian, an American, three Japanese, a German, and an Italian. I know. He told me."

"Well, where do you go when you go out?"

"There's a cinema, and a few restaurants. Not much."

"Would you like to go out sometime—I mean, you know, to the movies or something?"

"Yes," she said. "I'd love to."

They looked at each other and smiled. He was not usually very good at asking for dates, but this invitation had just appeared, as much a surprise to him as he imagined it was to her. She leaned back with her hands in the sand and he saw that her breasts were huge.

"How long is your vacation?" she asked.

"Three weeks."

"And then you go back to England? For how long?"

"Until June. In September I'm supposed to be going to college—I mean, university, what you call university. How old are you?"

"Twenty-six."

"Really?"

"Really. Does that make me seem old?"

"No. It just makes me feel young. Like a kid. I don't mean that to sound the way it sounds. Do you know what I mean?"

"Yes. You're a virgin."

He thought he blushed. "But I'm not," he lied.

"No?"

"No."

"How many times—"

"Once," he said.

"Were you in love?"

"Yes."

"Who was the girl?"

"Her name was Alice. I was staying with her family in Paris. I was supposed to be learning French, you know? Well, I didn't."

"Do you still love her?"

"Uh, I haven't seen her since last summer."

Mona looked at him, then opened *Balthazar* and continued reading.

His room was as sparsely furnished as a hotel room: a bed, a bureau, a chair, a small electric heater for the cold nights. His suitcase, overflowing with rumpled clothes, was still on the floor. On one of the white walls hung a map of Ireland, a gift from his grandfather. Sitting on his bed, he felt like a visitor waiting for someone to tell him what to do. His mother and father were both downstairs, napping in their bedroom. Quentin was off playing somewhere. In an hour or two it would be dark. Already the minaret calls were floating over the city—scratchy, fragmented prayers. Through one of his windows he could see across a dusty field to another row of stone houses. An abandoned, rusting Ford sat in the middle of the field. Through his other window he could see the embassy, a corner of the ambassador's house, the beach, the water. A clock was ticking downstairs in the living room.

He was thinking about Alice.

They had grown up together. They shared the same birthday. They had even once had nicknames for each other: he was Sebastian, she was Natasha. Her body must have touched his many times, but he had never noticed until it was soft in the moonlight in Paris, a dim whiteness standing by a green metal fence and lifting a pale, frightened face to be kissed. Then she had leaned on him, saying nothing, her rough, dark hair the horizon to a view of ferns, fence, rooftops, stars. He had felt her breasts, as she breathed, brush his chest, tentatively close. A car had passed by on the street beyond the fence, its headlights wheeling between the slats, and they both had started, stepping back and glancing quickly at the front door. It was closed. The curtained windows were a warm yellow. He had looked at her, filled his lungs with air, whispered her name—then stopped, at a loss, and kissed her again. This time their bodies had pressed together and her hands had stroked the back of his neck. Then she had straightened and said, "I suppose we should go in. They're probably waiting for us."

They had opened the front door and walked into the living room. The lights were on by the couch, and Timmy, Alice's younger brother, was sitting on the floor listening to "A Hard Day's Night." Mr. and Mrs. Taylor had come in, both wearing bathrobes, and they had all had a drink together.

"Well, Scobie," Mr. Taylor had said. "Do you still want to be a writer when you grow up?"

"Yes, sir."

"Scobie will never grow up," Mrs. Taylor had said, laughing. "Will you? Please don't."

Scobie had felt as if Alice were his wife, as if they were sitting with her parents as equals. The living room was beautiful to look at: a Picasso lithograph and a Cambodian tapestry on the wall, dark red books in the bookcases, marble ashtrays on the tables, an Isfahan rug on the floor, the soft light holding them all in a trance—his life had settled, arranged itself around this scene, held the image to its heart. But he had never slept with Alice. She was too shy, she had refused, and he had respected her too much to insist. Instead, they had sat together for hours, holding hands and kissing, until the summer was over and she returned to her boarding school in Switzerland and he returned to his boarding school in England. The next time he saw her she was wearing lipstick and having an affair with a banker.

Scobie left his bed and walked downstairs. Thin shadows stretched across the living-room floor. He could hear Hassan in the kitchen, and he could smell tea. He sat down in one of the armchairs and stared at the motes of dust dancing in the twilight. His body seemed suspended, detached from his mind. What he saw was more real than himself. The clock was ticking nearby and he sensed his parents behind their closed bedroom door. Hassan, singing to himself, filled the quiet house with a gentle, warbling chant. Scobie heard the kitchen screen door rattle open, bang closed, and Quentin's voice saying, "Hassan, I need some food."

"Food?"

"Yes."

"What kind food you want for?"

"Bread, I guess. And cookies. And fruit."

"Why?"

"It's a secret, Hassan. I can't tell anyone, not even you. Do you have a paper bag I can use? Thanks. Thanks a lot, Hassan. Bye."

The screen door slammed shut and there was a moment's silence in the kitchen, followed by a long sigh and more singing. Scobie rose and went outside. The sky was a pearly white, dazzling with sunset at the edge of the sea. He saw Quentin hurrying toward the beach. He was small and stout. Puffs of sand lifted and sank behind him. Scobie slowed down and took his time. The dust on the street lay molded by car tracks circling the identical houses. Neighborhood dogs ignored him as he passed them leaping up and down some sand piled against a wall. The road ran on between the barren gardens, past the long, low embassy. Then the beach stretched out before him, and he saw a dozen children, some standing with their hands on their hips, potbellied, bow-backed, and others sitting cross-legged in the sand. In their midst stood a tall, thin young man with a red beard. He was wearing a sheepskin coat and was leaning on a staff, talking to the children.

Scobie saw Mona resting against the side of an upturned fishing boat.

"Hello," he said. "What's this?"

"The children found him on the beach," she said. "His name's Phillip, I think. He's hitched all the way from England. Manchester. They've built him a little house— there, you see that lean-to? And they've all plundered their houses for food. It's quite exciting, actually."

Scobie looked back at the cluster of children. Whatever Phillip was saying, they were fascinated. They were silent, listening. Then, all at once, they were asking him questions.

"What did you do this afternoon?" Scobie asked.

"Oh, nothing. Watched the children. Read."

She was standing with her arms folded, and he realized she was self-conscious about her breasts.

"What're you doing tonight?" he asked.

"I have to take care of the kids. Mr. and Mrs. Marsh are going out."

"What about tomorrow night?"

"I'm not doing anything. There's a good film showing at the cinema, actually. A French film. It'll have Arabic subtitles, but that's all right. Rather baroque."

"What time?"

"I don't know. I'll check. I *think* it's a good film."

"Anything would be fun."

"Yes," she said, and laughed. "You're quite right."

It was growing dark. Phillip had unrolled a sleeping bag under his lean-to and made a small fire, over which he was now cooking something in a camper's frying pan. "Hot dogs." Mona laughed. The children sat in a circle around him, crouched on their haunches, watching.

"How old are you?" Mona asked.

"Seventeen," he said.

Mona sat next to him on the front seat of his father's green Chevrolet. The faint scent of her perfume drifted through the car. Pools of yellow light swept past the windows. On the left of the modern, empty highway leading into town was the desert. On the right was the sea. Mona was wearing a long maroon dress, a white shawl, and sandals. Already rings of sweat had formed under Scobie's arms, and he was sure he smelled like a gymnasium. They drove down Kuwait's main street, a wide boulevard with a strip of grass in the middle that had to be watered constantly, day and night. The sidewalks were crowded with outdoor cafés, each one illuminated by a television. As Scobie looked for a parking space, two dozen identical pictures of Mickey Mouse flashed simultaneously onto the screens. Below, Arabs in white *kaffiyehs* chain-smoked and watched.

The cinema, like the highway, was new, and it was packed with men. Scobie and Mona bought their tickets and sat near the front. They saw a newsreel, three coming attractions for Italian westerns, and twenty minutes of local advertising. Then the movie began. It was a French love story dubbed into English with Arabic subtitles, and had been so badly cut—every time a man and a woman even approached each other they promptly vanished—that it made very little sense. Halfway through, Scobie reached for Mona's hand. She returned the pressure of his fingers, without looking at him, and they held hands during the rest of the movie. Afterward, on the sidewalk outside, twenty or thirty men crowded around them, jostling each other and staring at Mona. She kept her arms folded and her eyes straight ahead. The men were almost hysterical with excitement, and Scobie thought there would be a riot and he would be clubbed to death. But they passed safely to the car, though a few men couldn't resist reaching out and pinching Mona's shoulders. She blushed and swore.

"Where to now?" Scobie asked, starting the car.

"Go back toward the embassy," she said. "There's a restaurant by the sea."

She sat close to him on the seat, quietly smoking a cigarette.

"What's that?" He pointed to a red hue in the sky above the desert.

"An oil fire," she said. "They're waiting for that famous fellow to come and put it out."

The restaurant was vacant and large, with candles on the tables and a plate-glass window overlooking the water. The moon was out again. They sat by the window, their feet touching under the table. She told him her father was a clerk, her mother worked part-time in a dress shop, and her two brothers, both older, were salesmen—Barnaby, the youngest, sold vacuum cleaners, Mason sold Austin Healeys. She had gone to school long enough to get two A-Levels, in art history and geography, before running away to Spain with a painter she met in a London discotheque.

"I lived with him for a year," she said. "Then with George, in Paris, and then with Peter, on Hydra, and then I worked in London for a while, and then I got fed up and answered an ad in the *Times* for a governess. And now here I am. I shan't stay much longer, I shouldn't think."

In the candlelight, her face was much softer, less intimidating, more relaxed. She leaned toward him with her elbows on the table.

"When I was a little girl I was convinced something special was waiting for me when I grew up. I didn't know what, but something very special, unique, I was con-*vinced*."

"And?"

"So far, nothing special." She laughed. "I didn't expect anything particular. That's why I do all the things I do. I say to myself, 'Well, it sounds daft, but this might be *it*.'"

In front of the Marshes' house, still in the car, he kissed her. Her lips were soft and warm, she opened her mouth, her tongue caressed his. They didn't hold each other tightly, they just sat with their hands touching and their heads leaning back against the seat.

"This is the nicest evening I've had in a long time," she murmured.

"Me, too."

"You're very gentle," she said, stroking his cheek with her fingers, her eyes a distant luster in the moonlight. "Very gentle."

Scobie had a small leather box, and in that box was a thin silver bracelet Alice had given him. He sat in bed, under the covers, with the bracelet on his knees, and thought of his brother Matthew, who was going to boarding school in the States and spending Christmas vacation with his grandparents on Long Island. Last Christmas, Scobie had been there. I should write him a letter, Scobie thought. He picked the bracelet up and looked at it closely. The house was quiet. Outside, the breathing desert—stars, moon, waves, moments of his life spinning and tumbling in space, or his head: the dry dust smell, dull tile, the sea, the blank blue sky, voices in the street, whispering. He put the bracelet in the leather box and turned off the lamp and looked at the slabs of light coming in the window and listened to the thrumming beach. The shadows of the objects in his room quivered before his eyes. He was not sleepy, only too tired to do anything but lie there in the dark dreaming of Mona. He rolled over and wondered if she were asleep yet. Or was she too lying awake, thinking? And if so, what was she thinking about? Or was she reading? Yes, she would be reading *Balthazar*. He tried to think of nothing but blackness, then whiteness, but words broke the serenity: *You're very gentle*. Was that a compliment? Was she laughing at him, for being young? Should he have touched her breasts, there in the car? Should he have been stronger? *You're very gentle*. What did that mean?

He sat up in bed, turned on the light, lit a cigarette, and rummaged around in his suitcase until he found a soiled spiral notebook. He opened the notebook to a blank page and wrote:

The embassy in Paris slowly drifts across my eyelids, droopy with the dust and the sun. Shoes move by, feetless. Billboards. Murmurs. Over the carefully planned garden and park, the distant music of cars. Waiting for a person, or a time, I forget, and watching two children playing. The smallest, a boy, chases his sister around and around a sandbox, making pig noises. A parasol walks by. The children are throwing sand at each other, but of course in the end they're playing together with a toy truck. Dresses rustle somewhere in my memory. I seem to recall their mother, tall and elegant. Her eyes were large and dark. The rest of her face was, I remember, too beautiful to be tender. She frequently paused before the various mirrors in her house, or glanced quickly at her reflection immediately upon entering a friend's house. Of course I never knew her. I have only seen her children, playing in the different streets of Paris, the long shady ones lined with hidden houses. I feel as if I were walking home from a party late at night, stopping and staring up at laughing couples leaning on balconies, or running my fingers along the layers of advertisement on a yellow wall—dating back, perhaps, to the last political crisis, or the transportation strike, or the birth of a bricklaying pop singer. It all passes, a million lives at once, while I sit on a painted bench watching some children and imagining their mother and . . . what? Waiting for Alice, I think. Yes, and here she comes, in a white raincoat, for some reason, to tell me, 'I'm having an affair.' An affair? At your age? With whom? 'A banker.' How old? 'Forty.' *Forty?* 'Yes.' Why? But I know. Because *I'm* not old enough. I should have slept with her last summer, but I didn't, because I'm a boy.

"I wish we could be alone somewhere," Scobie said.

"So do I."

The sun was reflected in Mona's green eyes. She lifted a handful of sand and let it slide between her fingers, the small pyramid dissolving, then collapsing. She stared at the children playing near the waves.

"I almost had a baby once," she said.

He had forgotten that such a thing was possible. "When?" he asked.

"Two years ago. But I had an abortion instead."

"That must have been very painful."

"It was. Psychologically."

"That's what I mean."

"And yet I wasn't prepared to have a child either. So . . ." She shrugged.

"Was the . . . father with you?"

"No."

"Why not?"

"He didn't know," she said.

"He *didn't?*"

"No. We had split up by then. That was Peter. I told you about him. We lived on Hydra together. Anyway, I didn't want to see him. He would have made a fuss. He would have wanted me to have the baby."

"Why?"

"Because it was his."

"I don't get it."

"You don't? Well, he was older than you. And he was very possessive. He would have considered it an *insult* for me to abort *his* child. Do you see?"

"Sort of."

"Oh, Scobie, you are naïve."

They were both silent for a while. Except for the children, they were alone on the beach again, but Scobie felt exposed, vulnerable; behind him were the windows of the ambassador's house and a wing of the embassy. An oil tanker moved slowly along the horizon. Mona was wearing a T-shirt, and Scobie could see the shape of her breasts clearly outlined in the striped cloth. Her bare feet were buried in sand. He wanted to reach out and touch her. He remembered the way her lips had covered his, last night in the car.

"Mona?"

"Yes?"

"Have you ever been in love, I mean really in love?"

"Several times." She laughed. "Have you?"

"I think so."

"With your girl friend, Alice?"

"Yes."

"Did she love you?"

"I don't know."

"Do you still love her?"

"I think about her a lot. Yeah, I guess I still love her a little."

"Have you ever been in love with anyone else?"

"No."

"It's not something that only happens once," she said.

"I know."

Suddenly she leaned over and kissed him, then sat back, smiling.

"What happened to that guy Phillip?" Scobie asked.

"Oh, he left for India this morning. He's looking for God, I'm afraid."

Veined and slender, his father's fingers cradled the miniature frigate and held it under the lamp. Papery planks and a brass cannon the size of a pearl gleamed as he brought his eyes closer, his horn-rimmed glasses mirroring the ship in a lake of white light. A cigarette was burning in the ashtray on his desk, next to a half-empty demitasse. Small tools lay scattered at his elbows. Behind him, hanging on the wall, was a faded watercolor of a sailboat at anchor. Smoke swirled up through the light and around his head. To his left, sitting on the couch, her knees tucked, was Scobie's mother, reading. As she read, her lips moved slightly, so that Scobie could almost hear the words. A Frank Sinatra album was on the Grundig, and his father suddenly started whistling along with the song, leaning back in his chair and scratching his cheek.

"Is Quentin over visiting Kathy?" Scobie asked.

"Yes," his mother said.

"I think I'll go see what they're doing."

"O.K. But tell him not to stay up too late."

"I'll tell him."

"And give my best to Mona," she said.

It was a cool evening, the moon and stars filling the sky. Scobie walked down the middle of the dirt road, between the stone houses and parked cars, until he reached the Marshes' house. A plump, blond-haired girl about ten years old answered the doorbell.

"Hi. I'm Quentin's brother."

"Oh, hi. I'm Kathy. Come in."

He stepped into a living room that was dark but for the gray light of a television screen. Dan Cartwright was hurriedly mounting his horse. Sweat trickled down Scobie's sides. He could barely see the shapes of small bodies sitting before the television.

"Is Quentin here?" he asked.

"Yeah. Hey, Quentin. Your brother's here."

None of the shapes moved.

"Actually, I was wondering if Mona's around," Scobie said.

"Sure. Upstairs."

"Upstairs?"

"Yeah. In bed."

"She's asleep?"

"Naw. She's sick."

"Sick?"

"Yeah."

"Well, um, where're your parents?"

"Out."

"Oh. Well, tell Mona I hope she's O.K."

"You tell her."

"Me?"

"Sure, just go up and tell her."

"Really?"

"Yeah, sure, why not?"

"Swift," he heard Quentin saying, somewhere near the television. "That was really swift."

"Well, how do I get there?" Scobie asked.

"Up the stairs, first right," Kathy said. "Just like your house. They're all the same."

"O.K. Thanks. I'll just go up for a couple of minutes and say hello."

"Sure."

He climbed the shadowy stairs to a dark hallway. He groped to his right. The door was open.

"Mona?"

He heard sheets rustling, then Mona's voice: "Who's that?"

"Me, Scobie. Are you asleep? If you're asleep, I'll go away."

He turned and started back down the stairs, his knees shaking.

"Scobie."

"What?"

"I wasn't sleeping."

"You weren't?"

"No."

"Oh, well, are you all right?" He returned to the hallway and peered into the black room. "Kathy said you were sick."

"Come here."

"Where?"

"Here, silly."

Reaching blindly into the room, he took a few steps forward and stopped. Her hand took his and guided him to the side of her bed. He sat down. As his eyes slowly adjusted to the darkness, he saw her bare shoulders above the sheets. Her fingers massaged his knuckles.

"Are you all right?" he whispered.

"Yes. What did the children tell you?"

"That you were sick."

"And what were they doing?"

"Watching television."

He could smell her body, the fragrance of perfume, and sweat, and something he couldn't identify, something almost bitter. Her hands slid up his arms to his shoulders, joined behind his head and gently brought him down to her mouth. What should he do? From a distance, he watched himself falter. He didn't know what to do. He started to unbuckle his belt, stopped, bent over and kissed her, his hands caressing her warm, supple body. His legs shivered. The house was suddenly quiet. Outside, a car door slammed.

"What's that?"

"Shhhh." She moved beneath him.

Something shuffled in the hallway.

"I heard something." He sat up.

She was still. "What?"

"I don't know," he whispered.

"There's nothing out there. Relax."

"Mona?"

"Yes?"

"I lied to you."

"You did?"

"Yes."

"About what?"

"Alice."

"Your girl friend?"

"Yeah."

"I don't understand."

"We didn't sleep together."

"You didn't?"

"No. I'm a virgin."

He heard her laughing softly in the dark. Then she sat up, brushing her hair from her face. "This is crazy," she whispered.

"I know. You're right. The kids could hear us."

"That's right," she said. "The Marshes could come home any minute."

"Yeah, you're right. Christ. This is crazy."

He buckled his belt and struggled into his shoes.

"Scobie?"

"Yeah?"

"Listen, you fool. Listen to me. Don't talk so much.

Hurry, button your shirt. Listen. *You're lovely.*"

She kissed him and pushed him toward the door.

Scobie dreamed they were walking through a city. She was ahead of him, wearing a long black dress. He called her name. She didn't stop. Again, he called her name. Still she would not respond. Running, he caught up with her, said her name, touched her on the shoulder, and turned her toward him. Then they were dancing in a large marble hallway. As they danced, she grew smaller and smaller, until she finally disappeared. He looked for her everywhere. He went to the Marshes' house, the beach, the embassy, the cinema. But he could not find her. The next day, he was told by Mrs. Marsh that she had taken the children to a Christmas party at the ARAMCO settlement. Around lunchtime, she was taking a nap, and not to be disturbed. "Remember," Kathy said. "She was sick last night." Scobie went back home and sat on the roof reading *Tender Is the Night.* It was siesta time, and the city was silent. It seemed that he was the only person alive. But Mona was there somewhere, only a few houses away. He thought about last night. It had happened so quickly. Why hadn't it seemed real? Why didn't it seem real now? He gave up reading and looked out over the city, then to the motionless sea, and wondered if he would ever wake up and touch the world.

"Why are you hiding?" Scobie asked.

"I'm not hiding," Mona said. "I just feel like being alone."

"But you hated being alone before."

"Well, I can't help that."

"Would you rather I left you alone?"

"Yes. Oh, Scobie. Just for now."

"I won't be here forever, Mona."

"I know." She sighed. "I know."

"Why do you want to be alone?" he asked.

"I can't explain."

"Oh."

"Don't be hurt."

"I'm not hurt."

"Good."

"Mona, I don't understand. Last night, I was practically in your bed."

"Scobie."

"What?"

"Who am I?"

"What do you mean?"

"Exactly what I said. Who am I?"

"Well . . . Mona."

"And what does Mona do?"

"She's . . . she's a governess."

"A *nanny*, Scobie. A *nanny*. And how old is nanny?"

"Oh, come on, Mona, that's irrelevant."

"Nanny is twenty-six. And how large is our community, Scobie?"

"Mona, will you please just—"

"Our community is the size of a small harem. All the old women talk. Buzz, buzz, buzz. Scobie?"

"What?"

"Do you understand now?"

"No."

"Then you're just being stubborn. And anyway, afterward you wouldn't want to see me anymore."

"That's not true."

"Yes it is. I know."

"How do you know?"

"I just do. I've been around. Admit it, you're relieved."

"What?"

"Admit you're relieved that you're free."

"I'm not."

"I don't believe you."

They were sitting in the Marshes' living room. The children were outside, playing in the yard. Mona sat on the couch. Scobie was in an armchair. He remembered how her eyes had looked when he had first met her: bright, laughing. Now they were dull and melancholy. Her arms were folded across her breasts. The sound of his breathing pressed against his ears.

"I just don't understand," he said.

"You will."

"Mona, I'm so sick of everything going through my life so fast."

She leaned forward and held his face in her hands. "Scobie, don't worry. Things will straighten out for you."

"I have to *have* something, Mona. I have to have something I can look at and think, 'That's my life.' You know?"

"I know. But listen. Take your time."

"I can't."

"You won't get it now, Scobie." She straightened. "I must see to the children. It's dinnertime. O.K.?"

She walked him to the door. Sunset slanted through the windows.

"See you later," he said.

Scobie's father came home from work and said, "We're going to Egypt. Oh, and there's a letter from Matthew." The minaret calls sang in the sky. His father whistled as he showered. His mother and Hassan laughed in the kitchen. Over dinner, Quentin said, "Scobie, Mona really likes you."

Scobie's mother and father looked at each other and tried not to smile.

"She told me," Quentin said. His large brown eyes watched Scobie intently. "Scobie?"

"Yeah?"

"Do you like her?"

"Sure," he said, glancing at his mother.

"What did you say to her last night?"

"Quentin, I think you'd better stop talking and start eating," his father said.

"Excuse me," Scobie said, standing and leaving the table.

Upstairs, in his bedroom, he lit a cigarette and stared at the pattern of green fish on his bedspread. Then he went out onto the roof and looked at the moon and cried, choked with sobs that rose from a sadness he had not known was so painful and deep. He longed to be a child again—sexless and voiceless and lost in the landscape, like the sea or the desert. And then, just as strongly, he wanted Mona. He wanted to feel her body next to his. He wanted to feel her hands on his back. He wanted to hear her sigh. He wanted to kiss her breasts, her shoulders, her face, her stomach, her cunt, her feet. He wanted to hear her saying his name.

He went inside and put on a sweater. His suitcase, he noticed, was still on the floor, only half-unpacked.

Scobie made himself walk slowly. He felt surrounded by a layer of air that magnified everything he saw: the silent white houses, the shapes of cars hunched at the curb, the suggestion of space between the high bright stars, the moon and its soft light, which merged, near the horizon, with the arched orange nimbus of the oil fire in the desert. Though there was a cold breeze, he was sweating; he raised his arms and let the current dry his shirt and sweater. It was a blue night out, and the objects around him seemed to swim in a sea. Toward how many girls' houses had he moved like this before? Leslie's, when he was ten, in hot, wet Baghdad. Dorothy's, in Rome, after following her through the set of *Ben Hur* and shaking hands with Charlton Heston. Alice's, returning from an afternoon in the Place de la Contrescarpe. The different girls and their different houses all formed a single radiant hue in his mind. He was walking along every street he had ever walked along; he was seeing everything he had ever seen. He was himself at every age. He had been here before. He had already seen this stone house approaching like a memory. Yet how was this possible? He had never been here before. He was a complete stranger. And he watched himself so carefully. He missed nothing. Not the chaotic long hair, or the self-conscious mouth, or the pimpled forehead, or the slouch, or the shuffle. He was inside himself and outside himself at the same time.

Mona opened the door. "Oh," she said.

"Hello," he said.

"Hello."

"I was wondering."

"Yes?"

"If you'd like to take a walk. It's a beautiful night."

"Scobie." She sighed. She was wearing a light cotton dress that reached her knees, and her hair was tied back in a bun.

"I'd like to talk to you, Mona."

"O.K. Just a minute."

She disappeared and returned with a shawl over her shoulders. "I can't be long," she said. "I left Kathy in charge."

"Do the Marshes go out every goddam night?"

"It's the holiday season," she said.

"Let's walk."

"Where?"

"Not far, to the beach or something."

"O.K." She laughed. "O.K."

She took his arm as they walked past the shadows of bicycles leaning against the houses. The embassy guards stiffened when they heard them coming, lifting their shoulders away from the backgammon table crammed inside their booth. A bare overhead light made them look like prison guards.

"Good evening," Scobie said.

He led Mona onto the beach, trying to ignore their smiles and curiosity.

"They'll leave us alone," he said. "Let's sit down."

"No. Let's keep walking."

"Mona?"

"Yes."

"I want to talk to you."

"All right. I'm sorry."

They sat down. The guards were lost behind the dunes. Curtains covered the windows of the ambassador's house. The moon flapped like a fish at their feet. He lay back in the cold sand and looked up at the sky. Mona sat with her knees drawn to her chin, staring at the water.

"What did you want to say?" she whispered.

He brought his hand up and touched her neck. He could not see her face. He touched her ear lobes, her cheeks.

She leaned back into his arms and kissed him. Her large lips were soft and pliant. His hands quivering, he touched her breasts beneath her dress. She closed her eyes, unsnapped his jeans, then sat back and pulled her dress over her head. Her moonlit breasts floated free. When her hands touched his naked skin he gasped. Pulling him down, she spread her legs, her knees bent. There was sand in their mouths as they kissed. Scobie was shivering uncontrollably. She brought him into the warm, wet center of her body, and her feet clasped behind his back. Heat flowed through him, moving in circles, in waves, out to his shoulders, his arms, his legs, his fingers, his feet. He was searching for a rhythm. He could not understand hers—

it was too slow, too luxuriant. He felt her legs tightening. "Slowly," she whispered. "Slowly, slowly, slowly." Different images, brief, almost subliminal memories, sped through his head. He saw himself as a boy, sitting on a bed, listening to the quick, sharp *plinks* of a piano being tuned. He could hear fishing boats outside, the stuttering of their small diesel engines lifting off the water and filling the narrow, shadowed space with the *pock-pock* of faraway tennis games, lawn mowers, electric saws, flying airplane models. Between the fishing boats and his room was the ragged thrust of island, where naked boys baked on the rocks and then dove into the fluted waves. Here and there the thud of dust, the heavy, measured beat of conversation, the flutter of eyelids staring out through the weight of sunlight to the sea, blinding and flat. Over everything lay the smell of skin warmed by sunlight, a child's skin. Intricate piercings of memory, something in the rhythm he now unconsciously found, drove through his skull like bullets: a Land Rover with its panels peeled by the seasons, a slumping black dog buried in a garden, an enormous red bicycle blistering on a terrace, a long stretch of rain, a dream, curiously detailed, a man with his hair on fire, an apartment in a city, a view of trees, two cats, a pair of riding boots in a closet, snatches of song, a car changing gears, a light slipping up one wall, across the ceiling and down another wall, ice cubes rattling in glass, twirling skirts, a statue slippery with moss, surrounded by pebbles, a sinking, a sinking—Mona touched his chin. He hissed, squeezing her waist, and fell into her arms, into the sound of her thumping heart.

He rolled over onto the sand. Mona's breasts were flat and round. Her stomach rose and fell gently. She watched the sky as if reading her own palm, her lips moving. Without a word, she rose and walked to the sea. The moonlight framed her against the dark waves. She ran the water over her body, bringing it up in her cupped hands and letting it splash down to circles at her feet. Scobie dressed and waited. She returned wet and shivering. He held out her thin dress. She pulled it on over her head and wrapped her shawl around her shoulders.

"I'm going home," she whispered. "I can't explain."

"Are you all right? Can't you come over to my place?"

"I should get back to the children." Her voice was quiet and sad. He held her shoulders and she looked up at him.

"Actually, I guess it is pretty late," he said.

"Yes."

"But I'll see you tomorrow, O.K.?"

"Of course."

"I'll walk you back."

"No, please, I'd rather go by myself."

"Are you sure?"

"I'm sure. Good night, Scobie." She kissed him.

"Good night."

He watched her walk across the sand, a thin shadow in the moonlight.

Her damp, sweet smell clung to his body. He gradually became aware of the sand in his hair and his teeth and his eyes, the pain low in his abdomen. He wanted to wash and lie down on a smooth bed and wait for the ache to subside.

When he could no longer see Mona, he counted to

fifty, then walked to the embassy gates. The two guards straightened and smiled, nodding as he stepped past them. His feet were light. He swaggered down the weaving road. He was alive, his whole body was alive, as if shocked by a perfect morning. Never had he felt so free.

"What happened to you?" his mother asked.

"What do you mean?"

"You're all wet and sandy."

"Oh, that. I, uh, fell into a mud puddle."

"A mud puddle?"

"Excuse me, I've got to go up and change."

"A *mud* puddle?"

He took a long shower, alternating the temperature of the water from hot to cold. He washed his hair, shaved, brushed his teeth, trimmed his fingernails, and stared at his face in the mirror above the sink, looking for changes. Then he went into his room and dried his hair. The small electric heater by the closet was glowing and clicking. The curtains were drawn. On his bedside table, a lamp cast a wide circle of light onto the ceiling. His parents were still awake downstairs. He could hear them talking. Humming to himself, he threw his wet towel onto the mound of clothing in his suitcase and climbed into bed. He lit a cigarette and reminded himself to write Matthew. He smiled. And Alice. He would write Alice and tell her he'd like to see her again. He would stop in Paris on his way back to boarding school, and she would meet him at the airport in a white raincoat, and he would—but then he thought of Mona. The memory of her touch, the lingering smell of her skin made him blush. A numbing regret replaced his happiness. He had not dreamed his ecstasies on the beach. The bodies had been real, his and hers, grappling like shadows in a fire. He felt his freedom slipping away. When he saw her tomorrow, what would he say? Would he sit with her on the beach, watching the children? Would he invite her to dinner, to eat at the table with his mother and father? Would he put on a tie and coat and take her to a party? No, he thought—instantly aged by the ease with which he wondered how he could possibly avoid her for the rest of his vacation.

The Slightest Distance

THE sun made Laura feel so heavy she did not believe she had the energy to rise and walk to the water. A drop of sweat snagged on her sunglasses, tickling her cheek. She brushed it away and looked up from her book.

Matthew sat next to her on the beach, also reading, his nose covered with Noxzema. Scobie lay beyond him, and beyond Scobie lay Quentin.

"Anyone for a swim?" she asked.

Matthew shook his head. "No, thanks."

"What time do we leave tonight?" Scobie asked, not opening his eyes.

"Four-thirty. Tomorrow *morning*."

"You're kidding."

"No," she said, then laughed. "So take a long nap after lunch."

Scobie groaned and rolled over onto his stomach.

Matthew's face, and Scobie's back, and Quentin's shoulder formed, in receding perspective, a single motionless statue.

Laura blinked and returned to her book. Not reading, she thought of Scobie; in the six months between last Christmas vacation and this summer he had changed. He had arrived in June too pale, too harried to be anything but unhappy. For six weeks he had said very little. Of course, this had happened before, but never before had she felt such a need to hear him speak. On past occasions she had simply waited, counting on his age, his growth, his changing personality to explain. But this time the situation seemed different. Maybe because he was eighteen, maybe because he was about to enter college, maybe because his reticence seemed more nearly permanent—whatever the reason, his silence now was painful.

She closed her book, picked up one of the boys' swimming masks, and quickly waded into the cold water.

The spoon lay at the bottom of the sea, a spark of silver swarming with fish. Fanning the water with her arms, she peered down through her mask at the specks of swirling light and for a second imagined that she was part of the sea, a flash of sponge or scale. Mysterious, diaphanous cells darted before her eyes. It seemed inconceivable that men plunged to the bottom in search of gold, plunged down to where even the light disappeared, down into that maze of rocks. She feared the cold layers of shadow. She feared drowning.

She lifted her face out of the water and pushed off her mask.

Her three sons were still on the beach. To their left, a fisherman sat mending his nets. Heat, quivering above the rocks, rose, the way the water descended, in layers. On the mountain, a donkey brayed. Matthew looked up from his book, saw her, and waved.

She waved back, and then, suddenly, without thought, she pulled the mask over her eyes, sucked in a lungful of air, and dove, kicking her way down toward the seaweed and sand. As she sank, the fear of drowning returned. She clawed for the spoon, but swirls of sand rose and obscured it from view. She kicked harder, forcing her body down, reaching in among the swaying silt and seaweed until she felt the metal touch her fingers. She grabbed but missed. Her lungs ached. Her arms moved slowly. Snapping her legs, she pressed herself down onto the bottom and dug for the spoon. Again she found it, and this time she held on, pulling it away from the rocks and up against her chest.

They were waiting for her on the beach, blankets and books under their arms.

"Look what I found."

"A spoon?" Scobie asked, leaning forward and staring.

"Yes."

"From where?"

"The bottom," she said.

"That's very interesting, Mom. A real find."

Matthew and Quentin laughed.

"*You* used to collect them," she said. "In Italy, remember?"

Scobie grinned. "Yes," he said. "I remember. Ice-cream spoons."

"That's right. So don't be so snooty."

"Mom, *hurry*," Quentin said. "It's lunchtime. I'm starving."

She pulled a white terry-cloth dress over her bathing suit, picked up her beach bag, and followed her sons toward the dock.

"Can you believe your father's finally coming?"

"No," Scobie said. "I can't. My theory is that we'll never see him again. He's disappeared for good. Up the Nile."

They walked along the edge of the water, where the sand was cool, until they came to the concrete steps leading up to the *taverna*—a two-story, whitewashed building that occupied a small section of rock jutting out into the harbor.

There was a terrace running along two sides of the *taverna,* covered with wooden chairs and tables and shaded by a green awning. Laura moved toward a table in the corner nearest the sea. A small boy in faded gray shorts and T-shirt was waiting.

"Hello, Yorgo," she said in Greek.

"Hello." He smiled.

"I think we'll have salad and fish today," she said. "And beer."

Yorgo disappeared into the building, his bare, brown feet slapping across the terrace.

Laura lit a cigarette and laid the silver spoon in the middle of the table.

"Remember when we used to dive for pebbles?" Scobie asked, picking up the spoon. "We thought they were pieces of gold. Remember?"

"Yes," Matthew said. "At Nana's."

"We used to dive for them the way you dove for this," Scobie told his mother.

The salad and beer arrived. They thanked Yorgo and started eating.

"You sure Dad will be there?" Scobie asked.

"He'll be there," she said. "Even he knows he needs a vacation."

The village of Mymeros was organized around the base of a mountain, rising to an ancient church and Venetian fort at the top. The sun reflected off the small, whitewashed houses as Laura and her sons, arm in arm, slowly climbed the slope. Occasionally an old Greek woman, shrouded in black, would peer from the shadowy interior of a house and wave.

Halfway up the mountain, facing the harbor, a green metal gate gave way to a series of stone steps that led down to the main floor of their house. A red-and-white tile terrace stretched along the front. Below the terrace were two levels of garden, then a wall. The view was of the sea, a few brown islands in the distance.

Laura crossed the terrace and walked into the front room. The shutters were drawn, and the room was shady and cool. She dropped her beach bag onto the floor, pulled off her dress and wet bathing suit, wrapped herself in a summer bathrobe, and lay down on her cot. She could hear her sons outside on the terrace, arguing about which tape to play on Quentin's tape recorder. From the harbor rose the gentle *put-put* of the island generator.

She could not sleep. She imagined that her sons had grown, that she had lost her children. When she was Scobie's age, she had fallen in love with his father. Now her son's and husband's voices were so similar she sometimes jumped when Scobie spoke. It was as if, at the age of forty-five, she were able to see Sam at eighteen—at any rate, see the body he had occupied. Staring at the intricate swirls of shadow on the ceiling, Laura wondered what it would be like when, years from now, she would visit Scobie's family, his wife and children, his house, his living room filled with books. It would happen, she knew; it was only a matter of time.

Her sons were quiet on the terrace. They had fallen asleep. The tape recorder was playing a song by the Beatles—"Here, There and Everywhere."

Two months ago the Egyptians had attacked the Israelis —or the Israelis had attacked the Egyptians—and she and Quentin had been put on a train, along with several hundred other Americans and Europeans, and taken to Alexandria. Sam had stayed behind, part of a small embassy staff that remained in Cairo. From Alexandria she and Quentin had traveled by boat to Greece, where Scobie and Matthew, on vacation from boarding school, had joined them. They had rented an apartment with a view of the Parthenon, high on Lykabettos; at night they could hear music from the Hilton rooftop nightclub. And then ten days ago they had come here, to this tiny island in the Aegean. For ten days they had been working on the house —painting the kitchen, clearing the garden, covering the outside walls with a fresh coat of whitewash. Tomorrow they would meet Sam in Rhodes.

One of the boys turned off the tape recorder and went back to sleep.

Laura tried to imagine what Sam was doing at this moment. If he had already arrived in Rhodes, he was probably napping, too. She could see him clearly, lying in bed reading *Motor Sport* or *Yachting*. She could see him showering, dressing in khakis and cotton shirt, and descending to the hotel bar with a book (*A History of the British Frigate*) in his hand. Of course, he could still be in Egypt; that had happened before. But she doubted it. She felt quite sure he would be there tomorrow. He would meet them at the dock. And then maybe *he* could talk to Scobie.

Like certain kinds of demonic music, the curve of Scobie's gaze, his bewildered resentment, bore into her and hurt. Scobie had never been prepared for life, though he had done more and seen more than most people his age. He dreamed too much. She sensed this dream but could not glimpse its contents. It had something to do with pride, a refusal to follow orders; though he denied it, he believed himself self-sufficient. Yet he looked at her as if to say, "Why *aren't* I self-sufficient?" And he was so romantic— like her, perhaps, he really did believe in the perfectibility of his future. Believed, but knew better, and so, caught between two perceptions, blamed her for the confusion. Life had not been like this when he was a child. Now— purposely, she suspected—he made things difficult for himself. He had never worked at school and so had been constantly threatened by expulsion, no college, a curtailed career. He seemed, despite himself, to thrive on threat.

Still, she would not have wished to change his life. At

least he felt the pain—there was that. At least he was aware.

Slowly, bodies from a dream, the three boys rose and stood with her on the terrace, watching twilight deepen across the water. The white houses glowed in the sun. Here and there a dark figure moved through a doorway, crossed the beach, called a name, waved. The rocks of the island were red—luminous and shifting, as if dangling from a mobile.

Matthew spoke first. "I'm going for a swim."

"It's too cold," Scobie said.

"No, it's not. Quentin?"

Quentin nodded and stood; he and Matthew disappeared into the house to change.

Scobie and Laura remained on the terrace, sitting in green canvas chairs and gazing at the sunset.

"It's kind of spooky, this time of day," Scobie said.

"That's what your father thinks."

"He does?"

"Yes. He says it depresses him."

Matthew and Quentin crossed the terrace on their way to the gate, both in bathing suits and sweaters.

"Don't be long," Laura said.

"We won't."

The gate clanged shut behind them.

She looked down at the harbor and saw the first fishing boat pull into shore, the sun reflecting off its cabin windows.

"Mom."

"Yes?"

"Has Dad been in any danger?"

"A little."

Scobie rubbed his hands across his shoulders. "Is he mad at me?"

"For what?"

"For, I don't know, school—all that."

"No. He's sorry you're not happy, that's all."

"I'm happy."

"You are?"

"Yes. I feel like I'm missing something, but that's not unhappiness."

"What do you feel you're missing?"

"I don't know." He shrugged.

"I mean, a person, or a . . . thought, or what?"

"A person, I guess. Maybe a thought. A *clearness*."

"To see?"

"Yes. And hear, taste, touch, smell. The works." He paused. "I feel very distant," he said.

"Distant?"

"Yes. From myself."

It seemed to her that his words ballooned out and allowed her to see, for the first time that summer, something of his dream. "You think of yourself as 'he'?" she asked.

"Yes," he answered, surprised. "That's right."

"You *are* like your father."

"I am?"

"In many ways. Sometimes I think he still feels distant from himself."

"He doesn't act it."

"Oh, you don't know." She watched Scobie light a cigarette. "He thinks a great deal of you," she said.

Scobie was silent, staring off to sea. She noticed a thin line above his lip; he was growing a mustache.

"He'll be glad to see you," she said.

"He doesn't talk much."

"No. Neither do you."

He looked at her. "Is that true?"

"What?"

"That I don't talk very much?"

She laughed. "Yes, my dear. You are the silent type. The brooding poet."

He laughed, too, shyly revealing his large, bright teeth. She borrowed his cigarette and lit one of her own.

"Do we have to go to this party tonight?" he asked.

"Yes. It would be impolite not to. Anyway, it will be fun."

"They're celebrating a saint?"

"Yes." She picked a piece of tobacco off her lip. "I remember, years ago when we lived in Athens, your father and I went to a wedding on Mykonos. It was very funny. For a long time everybody just sat around on stiff chairs, the women on one side of the room, the men on the other. But when the wedding was over, the entire island celebrated for twelve hours. I can barely remember myself swaying on the back of a donkey, in the middle of a long line of donkeys winding their way down a mountain path. It was night. Before me and behind me spread a beautiful flickering—dozens of candles. Each rider of each donkey held a candle in his hand. I was quite drunk."

"Look."

She followed his pointing hand and saw her other two sons on the beach below. The sand was in shadow and the water was gray-red and still. Matthew and Quentin were racing, their hair flying out behind them. Every few yards they pushed each other and laughed. The shaking sound of their laughter carried up to the terrace where she and Scobie sat watching.

Laura and her sons reached the top of the mountain just as the sun disappeared into the sea. Strings of electric light bulbs hung in canopies above the open square. Most of the villagers had already arrived. Their voices excited her; she felt the contagious spirit of a festival and clapped her hands. Scobie grinned. Matthew and Quentin, walking ahead, turned and urged them on.

"Dionysus," Scobie said, pointing to a well-muscled young man leaning against the side of the church. He was dark from the sun and dressed in gray cotton trousers and a starched white shirt. He stood perfectly still.

"Where do we go?" Matthew asked.

"I don't know," she said. "Over there, by the wall."

A ring of wooden chairs had been set up with their backs to the view, facing the square. The four of them nudged through the crowd and sat down.

A tall fisherman approached with glasses of retsina in his hands.

"For us?"

"Yes," he said, his dark mustache bobbing above his smile. "For you."

They each took a glass and saluted him. He bowed, smiling, and vanished into the crowd.

"Cheers," Scobie said.

The musicians tuned their bouzoukis and began to play. Immediately the square was filled with the young men of the village, dancing together in a circle. The older men and women and children stood back, watching and clapping. Bottles of retsina passed from mouth to mouth. Soon the young men were in a frenzy, leaping and slapping the ground, clapping their hands, then springing and kicking into the air like acrobats.

Beyond the perimeter of electric lights it was dark. Laura drew her sweater up closer around her neck and took a swallow of wine. Scobie, his elbows on his knees, was watching the dancing. Matthew, twisted sideways on his chair, was watching the thin horizon streak and diminish. Quentin was also watching the dancing, his glasses halfway down his nose.

She looked at Scobie, then away, embarrassed. This was a man sitting beside her. *Her son.* So much time, and all of it invested in this body—was it a crime to waste youth on youth? Sometimes she thought so. Sometimes she resented Scobie for being her son, just as he surely resented her for being his mother. Soon Matthew would be a man. Then Quentin. Three sons, three departures.

The dancers were waving at her—no, at her sons; they were beckoning her sons into action.

"Go on," she said. "Dance."

Reluctantly, they rose and walked onto the square. Shoulders parted, large brown hands pulled them in, and the music resumed, her sons—flying, bewildered, self-conscious, out of step—joining the dancers.

Laura sipped her retsina. Nostalgia plagued Scobie, she knew, as much as it plagued her. But why? Because he traveled so much? Because each moment of his life, a fragment, was too brief to be real, therefore always beautiful? With her it was simply an awareness of all that had gone before, all that she had already passed through—every scent and gesture caught forever. Perhaps it was the same for him. Perhaps the "something" he missed had already come and gone. She didn't know. She could only guess, and it made her sad to think such mysteries permanently mysterious, perhaps deceiving, perhaps—this was the worst —unsolvable.

"Missis?"

She looked up into the dark, smiling face of the young man she had seen earlier—Dionysus. "Yes?"

"Please . . ." He made a loose, uncertain gesture of his hands, smiled, and waited.

"Of course," she said.

He sat down.

She pulled a cigarette from her pack and immediately the young man had his lighter out and sparking.

"Thank you."

"Welcome."

They sat back and stared at one another. He looked about twenty-four, handsome, competent at something— carpentry or fishing. She offered him a cigarette.

"Win-ston," he said, smiling and flicking his lighter. "Very good."

"What is your name?" she asked.

"Kosta."

"Do you live on this island?"

He shook his head, and pointed toward the sea. "Cos." Then, puffing deeply on his Winston, he asked, "What is your name?"

"Laura Richardson."

"Rich-ard-son." He repeated the name.

"Those are my sons," she said, nodding at the dancers.

"Very nice sons," Kosta said. "Very wonderful boys, Mrs. Rich-ard-son."

"You speak good English," she said.

He beamed. "Thank you very much."

A bottle of retsina came their way. Kosta poured some into her glass, took a swallow from the bottle, then passed it on. He wiped his mouth with a clean white handkerchief.

"You have no . . . husband?" he asked.

His nonchalance betrayed him; he *was* flirting.

"Yes," she said, firmly. "I'm going to see him tomorrow."

Kosta looked at her sadly, his beautiful brown face shimmering beneath the swaying electric lights. She smiled.

"Ch-*rist*." Scobie collapsed into his chair.

"Welcome back," she said.

"Mother, I swear to God, I think I'm dying."

She laughed. "You're getting flabby."

"I beg your pardon, but those guys are freaks. They've got springs instead of legs."

Matthew and Quentin jumped from the circle and returned to their seats. Quentin's glasses were misty and askew.

"My sons," she said.

"How do you do." Kosta rose and shook their hands. "Very nice to meet you."

"Your name?"

"Kosta."

"Hi, I'm Scobie. That's Matthew, and Quentin."

"Sco-bie. Mat-hew. Kenton."

Scobie grabbed another passing bottle of wine and they each took a long swallow.

"Mom, you should dance," Matthew said.

"Women don't dance."

"Sure they do."

"Your mother, she is an excellent dancer?" Kosta asked, smiling.

"Fantastic. Just terrific. Incredible."

"Oh, Scobie, stop."

"Hey," Matthew said. "Something's happening."

She looked into the square and saw that all but an old man in blue jacket and baggy brown trousers had drawn back from the circle. His feet were bare and flat, his hair thick, white. Slowly he crouched, his arms spread at his sides, and began to dance. The musicians caught the tempo and played along. He snapped his fingers and sprang straight up, magically tall, then came down in a lower crouch, his feet shooting out before him, his heels slapping the stone, and danced as if, with age and speed, he could spin the entire island out to sea.

"Mom?"

It was Scobie, still awake on the terrace.

"Yes?" Laura paused in the doorway.

"Was that guy flirting with you?"

"Yes."

"I thought so."

"Go to sleep," she said. "In four hours you have to get up."

"It's almost not worth it."

"Every little bit helps."

"Mom?"

"What?"

"Did you like him?"

"Who?"

"That guy, Kosta."

"Very much," she exclaimed, surprised at herself. "Very much."

She awoke with the alarm clock in her hands. It was still dark. The only sound was the island generator and a few isolated waves at the mouth of the harbor. She sat up, reached for the light, turned it on. The sudden brightness made her blink. She pulled on her bathrobe and walked out onto the terrace. "Boys."

They didn't move.

"Time to get up. Scobie, arise. You're just in time for dawn."

"Mother, for Godsake . . ."

"It's time to get up."

Like a robot, Matthew suddenly jerked to a sitting position, snorted, and stood. "Good morning," he said.

The light was now gray. They could see each other. Quentin was still zipped into his sleeping bag, a small breathing hole the only sign of life. Scobie slowly propped himself up on his elbow and watched with her and Matthew as the distant edge of the sea grew a faint, faint red.

"How long do we have?" Scobie whispered.

"Half an hour. Wake your brother and let's get ready."

She returned to the front room and opened her suitcase. She packed her nightgown and bathrobe, the alarm clock, and the book by the cot. Then, dressed, she carried her suitcase out to the terrace. *"Quentin!"*

The lump shook, gasped, and a hand came poking through the air hole, fingers groping for the zipper. The bag opened. Quentin sat up and stared at his knees.

"Get dressed," she said.

She left him sitting on his cot and walked to the outhouse, a small stone building by the garden wall. The door was blocked by Scobie, who was swearing.

"What's wrong?"

"The damn thing won't flush."

"Oh, Scobie, please."

"Mother, it just won't *flush*. It's not my fault."

He straightened and stepped out.

"What shall we do?" she asked.

He pointed to the garden.

"No, I mean, we can't just leave it like that."

"We'll have to."

"Scobie, we cannot just leave it like that."

"We'll tell the mayor. He's awake for every boat. We'll tell him at the dock."

"All right."

Matthew and Quentin were dressed and waiting on the terrace.

"Everybody ready?"

"Should I bring my tape recorder?" Quentin asked.

"Yes," Scobie said. "O.K.?"

"O.K. Let's go."

They picked up their suitcases, closed the gate behind them, and began the walk down the mountain. It was almost daylight, yet she could not see the sun. Roosters crowed all across the island. A single dog barked. Laura and her three sons, forming a single, silent line, wound their way between the ice-blue houses.

At the bottom of the mountain they found a small group, including the mayor, sitting at a table on the *taverna* terrace, waiting for the ship.

Laura nodded hello and sat down.

A sleepy Yorgo brought them small glasses of hot tea and biscuits.

"Mr. Mayor?"

The mayor turned and smiled. He was a large, round man with a bald head and anxious, startled eyes. He owned the only grocery store on the island. "Yes, Mrs. Rich-ard-son?"

"Our toilet."

"Toilet?"

"Doesn't work."

"Doesn't work. Does-ant work." He shook his head, staring at the table. "Doesn't work?"

"Is broken," Scobie said.

"Ah, *broken*."

"Yes," she said.

"No worry, have *no* fear. Everything will be fixed." He smiled.

Silently, they sipped their tea and waited for the ship. The sky was beginning to turn the color of mother-of-pearl. Some fishermen appeared and ate their breakfast, then began loading their nets into their caïques. Roosters crowed through the village.

"There it is," Quentin said.

What looked like a string of floating electric lights appeared around the edge of the harbor. Gradually, the ship itself materialized—a long white phantom. A whistle blasted and then the anchors splashed into the water, chains rattling loudly in the still dawn.

"Let's go," Scobie said.

They picked up their suitcases and followed the small crowd down to the dock.

One of the fishermen had his caïque ready to take them out to the ship. Scobie jumped aboard, then helped his mother. Matthew and Quentin handed him the suitcases and climbed aboard themselves. The only other passengers were an old man and woman sitting on either side of their wicker suitcase, waving goodbye to somebody on the dock.

"Don't worry, Mrs. Rich-ard-son!" the mayor called, a hat covering his baldness. "Everything is fixed."

She waved. "Thank you."

The caïque pulled away from the dock.

"Don't worry, Mrs. Rich-ard-son!" the mayor screamed. "Everything is O.K.!"

She turned and faced the nearing ship. Warm, salty air blew across her face. When the giant hull was only twenty yards away she swiveled and looked back at the island, the village spread across the mountain, and the sun—there it was—exploding in the sky. At the top of the mountain the dome of the old church caught the first rays and turned pink.

The sky was high and blue, the sea calm. Laura sat in a deck chair on the port side of the ship, watching the islands slide across the horizon; it seemed they were moving, not the ship. In her left hand, resting on her knee, was a glass of tea. She was smoking a cigarette. Matthew sat in the deck chair next to hers, reading. Three seagulls squawked and circled above the wake of the ship.

"Do you realize that Ulysses might have seen this view?" she said.

Matthew looked up from his book. "I know," he said, squinting at the sea. "He probably did."

She looked at him. "What are you reading?"

"Seferis," he said.

She sipped her tea. "He won't write anymore," she said. "Why not?"

"Because of the government, the colonels. It's his way of protesting."

"I'm sure the colonels could almost give a damn."

"They do, I bet. Bad publicity hurts."

"Maybe."

A Greek in a tight gray suit passed them, nodding and smiling, and disappeared down the steps to the lower deck.

"Where's Quentin?" she asked.

"Asleep," Matthew said.

"And Scobie?"

"Trying not to be sick."

They both laughed.

"Where?"

"In the bar, I think," Matthew said. "Writing."

"He's the only one of you who still gets seasick." She laughed again.

"Mom, why is he so irritable all the time?"

"He's not irritable *all* the time."

"But you know what I mean."

"Yes."

"Why?"

She shrugged. "He's eighteen. He's about to go away to college. He's independent."

"I don't understand."

"I don't either, honey." She stood. "I'm going to find him."

He was in the bar, at a small table near a window. Before him was an open notebook and an empty coffee cup. He looked up as she approached. "Hello, Mother."

"Hello." She sat down next to him. "How are you feeling?"

"O.K. But I'll feel a lot better when I get off this boat." He lit a cigarette and looked out the window.

"Are you excited about seeing Dad?" she asked.

"Yes."

"Me, too."

"I just hope he's there."

"He'll be there."

Scobie smiled. "You have such faith, Mother."

"He'll be there," she said.

They each ordered a cup of coffee—Nescafé—and then sat waiting as it cooled.

"What are you writing?" she asked.

"A story," he said, closing the notebook.

"About what?"

"Nothing."

Scobie turned and looked at her; his mustache was already heavier, thicker.

"Remember what I said about missing something?" he asked. "Well, it's the same with writing. It's never quite right."

"You're young."

"Yeah."

"Don't be so impatient."

He lit another cigarette, gently placing the cold match in the saucer of his coffee cup. "Mom, tell me about Dad."

"What do you want to know?"

"What he was like when he was young—my age."

She leaned back and stared across the bar. There was a young woman by the opposite window, holding a crying baby.

"He was like all of you," she said.

"All of us?"

"Yes. I can see something of him in each one of you."

"When Matthew and I used to visit Nana, she would tell us all about him. One time she drove us to his old high school and showed us the field where he played football. She said she used to come to pick him up after school, and she could always tell it was him because she could hear him whistling."

"That was before I knew him."

"And when you knew him?"

"He still whistled. He didn't play football, but he still whistled."

"He wanted to paint, didn't he?"

"He did paint."

"Why did he stop?"

"He still paints," she said.

"Not seriously."

"I don't know," she said. "He still paints very well."

"But not all the time, Mother. He's not a *painter*. He's a diplomat. Why?"

"Maybe he didn't think he was good enough, or maybe he just didn't think he could support himself painting."

"O.K. That's what I want to know. I mean, could it be that he wanted to fill his life with events—you know, things happening, rather than watching, painting?"

"Yes," she said. "That could be."

"Maybe painting depressed him in a way. Like twilight. Maybe he *cured* himself, you see, by refusing to paint."

"He didn't cure himself," she said.

Matthew tapped on the window, waving them outside. They left the bar and walked onto the deck. Quentin was there, sitting in a canvas chair listening to his tape recorder:

> Cellophane flowers of yellow and
>   green,
> Towering over your head.
> Look for the girl with the sun in
>   her eyes,
> And she's gone.

Rhodes was nearing, a sharp blaze of stone and beige soil, olive trees and crumbling walls. Laura and Matthew and Scobie stood at the railing and watched as the island slipped closer and closer. Their ship rounded a peninsula of rock and the city came into view—white houses brilliant in the sunshine. Entering the mouth of the harbor, the ship's whistle gave a startling shriek. Laura pressed closer against the railing, searching the dock for Sam.

"Do you see him?" she asked.

Scobie shook his head.

She looked back at the dock. It was crowded with people and carts. The confusion was intoxicating. She felt herself clapping again, like a child. Voices called out in Greek, laughed and shouted. Then she saw him. He was standing by a coil of rope, dressed in khakis, sandals, and pale-blue shirt. As she watched, his forefinger nudged his glasses back up his nose. He had lost weight. He was skinny. She waved, but his eyes could not pick her out among all the other passengers. He was staring right at her but he could not see her. She waved again, then suddenly felt herself crying. At the same moment Scobie, clear and tall in the sunlight, stood on his toes, smiled, and waved.

"Mom, look. I see him."

Photographs

THE island was attached to the mainland by a long stretch of sand. Slowly it was civilized, first by Indians, who came to fish in the summers, and then by white men, who built mansions among the trees and brought their families out from the city. The women, planting flowers, discovered arrowheads. The reeds were cleared until each house had a beach. Yachts, moored offshore, revolved on their anchor lines, brass fittings winking in the sunlight. A tomahawk was found in the graveyard. Elizabeth, Matthew Duy's oldest daughter, married Quentin, Kenneth Richardson's oldest son, and a new house was built on the tip of the island, facing south. Because the house was exposed to the wind, it was very cold in the winter. Elizabeth planted roses and hung wicker birdcages from the trees. Quentin raised golden retrievers and won trophies, hunted duck, quail, and pheasant. By the time Sam was born, the civilizing was over. Twenty-four mansions lined the single road that ran down the middle of the island. Men hired from the village nearby kept the oak trees and apple trees and elms and evergreens pruned, the lawns and hedges trimmed, the leaves raked, the windows polished. Gardeners continued to find arrowheads in the soil, some of which they kept, some of which they turned over to their employers. Sam explored the island. He built model boats, airplanes, and cars, followed the pheasants and squirrels back and forth across the lawn, and listened to "Captain Midnight" on the radio. When he was nine, Ken was born. The stretch of sand connecting the island to the mainland became a public beach. The nearby village became a resort. But in the autumn, after the vacationers had left and before the snow had fallen, the island looked much the way it had when the Indians first came to fish. The sand was clean and white, the water sparkled like a handful of gold coins, and the houses were very quiet behind the trees, as if no one lived in them. Sitting outside one afternoon, watching a squirrel chase a walnut, Sam smelled the smoke of the next-door neighbor's burning leaves and knew that someday he would have to go. The smoke, the small white cloud rising through the trees, seemed a signal. His mother was on the terrace, watering flowers. Out on the water a single sailboat slid through the sunlight.

There were two hurricanes—the first in 1938, when Sam was in high school, the second in 1944, when Sam was home from college for Christmas vacation. It was as he and his father were standing at the window, watching the wind tear and claw at the old oak trees outside, that Sam took out his pipe and lit it. He heard his mother, sitting on the couch behind them, gasp. His father simply turned, stared for a moment, and then calmly looked back out the window, smiling.

Scobie, two years old, watched his grandmother crochet an afghan of reds and greens. Her small hands plucked and soothed the yarn. She showed him her collection of spoons and a three-legged squirrel. Her rings, green, flashed as she stood by the window, pointing: "There, see him?" Scobie discovered the island—at first alone, then with Matthew and Quentin. His grandfather swallowed Oreos with one hand and pulled them out of his ear with the other hand. When Scobie's family moved to Greece, his grandmother came to visit, adding the Eiffel Tower and the Parthenon to her collection of spoons. His grandfather would not come, because the airplane hurt his ears. One morning Scobie told his grandmother, "Fish is my hatest." She never forgot, reminding him even as he grew older that fish was his hatest. He called her Nana, his grandfather Pa.

Curtains fluttered as the breeze, smelling of salt and mowed grass, came in through the windows overlooking the sea. Nana kept the arrowheads she found in a little box on her bureau. Pa had an owl stuffed in the city; it hung, green and blazing, on the wall of his den. The island moved, shifted. Some of the beaches grew longer, some shrank. Here and there the reeds reappeared. When the entire family gathered for holidays, Nana would say, "It's just like a dream. I can't believe it's happening." The men played golf and the women croquet. A fact was mentioned, calmly, between strokes: "We found this country, built her up from nothing, made her what she is today. Certain unnamed peoples wish to destroy everything we have labored to create and it is our responsibility to stop them." Scobie imagined his father hesitating halfway across an Egyptian courtyard, reminded of something by the cooing doves and trickling fountain. "All the birds have gone for the winter," Nana would write. "But they'll be back in the spring."

The island shifted another inch, stretching the sand. Scobie remembered the summer he discovered an arrowhead, the summer he and Matthew went to the circus. There was a third hurricane, in the autumn of 1960, which destroyed one of the oaks and covered the beach with oil.

The view from the front window was cluttered with boats. The bay was dredged, and refuse poured in until the water turned brown and the beaches gray. In the attic Scobie found a Civil War sword, a photograph album, and a pair of lace-up shoes. One summer, he attended debutante parties in the mansions along the tree-lined road, dressed in a suit Nana purchased for the occasion. She told him, "You look so much like your father," and "You can be proud to be a Richardson."

In the photograph album, Nana was an eighteen-year-old bride, with a small, delicate chin and defiant eyes. She sat on a beach, a large sun hat at her side, smiling into the camera. She was squinting against the sun, her hand raised to shade her eyes. The gesture gave her a startled look, as if she had just seen something unexpected off to the left of the photographer. On the next page, Pa was standing in a field with Scobie's father. They were both dressed in Abercrombie trench coats and business hats. Pa cradled a shotgun in his arms. Looking closely, Scobie saw that his grandfather was on the verge of laughing aloud, and that, in the distance, golden retrievers paced impatiently. It looked cold—a gray day in late autumn.

Scobie came home from a Christmas party one night and found Pa on a stool before the fireplace, burning a boxful of letters and photographs. The paper wavered for a second on the uppermost log, then suddenly caught and curled at the edges, an ashy blackness slowly obliterating the faces and addresses.

In the spring of his freshman year in college, Scobie went to visit his grandparents. They were waiting for him at the station. He watched from the upper level as they approached—Pa edging through the crowd like a boxer, shoulders tucked, feet shuffling, and Nana following at his side, tugging his sleeve, waving, pointing, waving again. The loudspeaker called "Philadelphia" and a time, and then she was there, squinting, waving, patting her hair, her dress, her hair, reaching up and pulling him down to her cheek—a touch and smell so familiar he quickly straightened and shook hands with his grandfather.

Outside, as they waited for Pa to return with the car, Nana tugged at the hair on his shoulders and asked, "Don't you want to get this cut?"

A taxi blared by. "Not particularly," he said.

She tightened her mouth, a quick, pouting lift of the lips. "For me?" Fine silver bracelets rattled on her wrists.

Scobie looked off toward the parking lot. An airplane flew overhead, red and blue tail lights blinking in the dark.

Pa drove the silver-blue Chevrolet cautiously, in the right lane, eyes narrowed by the oncoming headlights. Following the curve of the coast, they approached the island. The car hit the bump that had been at the beginning of the road for as long as Scobie could remember. The headlights swung across the trees, picking out the mailboxes and name plaques. Gravel crunched as they pulled up the driveway. Scobie stepped out into the sound of crickets and pine branches. Nana climbed out behind him. "Well," she said. "Here we are. Home." The old Greek cowbell swayed and rattled as Pa opened the front door. The hallway smelled of lavender and dust. In the kitchen, the refrigerator clicked. Squirrels ran across the roof.

When Scobie was in bed, Nana came into his room, leaned forward once again, down toward his face in the darkness, and whispered, "Please, cut your hair. Tomorrow. For me."

The gravel driveway linking the house to the rest of the island twisted in small, sectioned curves toward the mailboxes. The oaks and evergreens and heavy apple trees uncurled in the bright morning air. The leaves were wet and spongy, hissing gently as they dried. Behind Nana and Pa's house was an older house, one of the first built on the island. Now it was empty, but not too long ago two aunts had lived there, two laughing ladies who would sit at a table on the lawn, eyes shaded with sun hats, and knead wet clay into ashtrays and cups. The mailboxes at the end of the driveway always contained more newspapers and advertisements and bills than letters. In the hallway, next to the potted palm, there was a mother-of-pearl cigarette box from Jerusalem. Looking up through the complex net of branches toward the sky, Scobie could see two knots of rope on the largest oak tree—all that remained of the swing Pa had given him ten years earlier.

Another photograph showed Nana and Pa standing together on the deck of a yacht. They were holding hands, smiling. The yacht was moored in front of their beach. Over their shoulders Scobie could see the house, the large front window through which, looking up, he now saw his grandfather walking across the lawn with an armful of dead branches.

At the end of the lawn was a toolshed—a damp, dark room that reeked of kerosene and wet dogs. Two lawnmowers filled the floor. Rakes and shovels hung from the walls. In the corner near the door was a summer life preserver, a plastic, deflated horse. Behind the croquet set was an old black flipper. No dogs slipped through the hatch that led to the kennel. An airplane passed low overhead, the drone slowly fading into the distance. Below the toolshed, on the beach, was a well that squirted fresh water into the reeds, and the skeleton of a duck boat buried in the sand. A single buoy bounced on the waves. Near the only boulder on the beach, hidden beneath the sand, was the fort Scobie and Matthew had built as boys—six fist-size stones neatly lined in a double row.

In the kitchen, Nana would point to the sink and say, "Don't you think the way the light comes in there should be a painting?"

"A what?" Pa would ask.

"Painting."

"It's just a sink, that's all."

"Oh, but dear, look at the light. It's so beautiful this time of day."

Later, after Pa had left, she would say, "You have to try and understand him. He doesn't mean what he says."

Through conversation Scobie learned that she had taught him how to walk and that once, in the twenties, she had danced with a prince in the Bahamas. But when he asked her why she didn't paint anymore, she just shook her head and sighed. "You're right. I should. But I just can't sit still long enough." Or she said, "I don't have the materials anymore. I gave them to your father."

The island never had a newspaper of its own, but the nearby village paper occasionally carried articles on the comings and goings of its neighbors. In a copy of Nana's Bible, Scobie found a clipping that showed his entire family standing on a dock. The side of a huge ocean liner rose behind them. Nana wore a skirt that reached way below her knees and a wide hat with a veil. Scobie and Matthew were looking at each other, not the camera. Their father had his hands on their shoulders. Pa looked very proud.

A week after Scobie graduated from college and two days before he left for a summer in Europe, Nana touched his knee and said, "It's so nice to have you home."

"What are you going to do now that you've graduated?" Pa asked.

"I don't know."

"What are you going to live on? Air?"

"I'll be all right."

"More potatoes, dear?" she interrupted.

"No thanks. Pa, what happened to your boat?"

"Stolen."

"Oh, I'm sorry."

"Why would anyone do a thing like that?" Nana sighed.

"Money," Pa said. "Same reason they do anything."

"I just think it's so *mean* for someone to do a thing like that," she said. "What plate do you have, dear?"

Scobie looked. "The train."

"Your favorite."

"Yes."

"How you loved that when you were a little boy."

Later, she came to the bedroom and stood in the doorway, plucking her sweater, peering. "You should go to bed, dear."

"Yes."

She moved closer. "Are you writing?"

"Yes."

"What?"

"A letter."

"Oh."

She turned down the bed, smoothed the sheets. "Don't forget," she whispered. "He doesn't mean what he says."

"That's all right."

"You'll get your hair cut? Tomorrow?"

"Sure."

"Good night, dear."

"Good night."

Scobie undressed, climbed into bed, and turned off the light. He was in the darkness, a part of the darkness, for a long time. He heard his grandfather shuffle up the stairs, snapping a light switch at the far end of the hallway. Pipes rattled and cleared themselves in some lower region of the house.

She died in the middle of the night, suddenly, without warning. She simply stopped breathing. Pa crumpled too, not dead but tired. She was burned. She wished her ashes to be spread across the water. Scobie and Matthew sat beside the living-room window with their father and grandfather and Ken, watching snow cover the apple tree. A squirrel high-stepped through the snow. The refrigerator clicked in the kitchen.

"In the twenties, she was a flapper," Scobie said.

"No," Sam said. "She just dressed like one."

It was very cold, so they built a fire in the fireplace and boiled water for tea.

"I knew she'd died," Scobie said. "I felt it."

Pa turned the pages of *National Geographic* and cleared his throat.

They had dinner with the rest of the family, aunts and cousins taking her place in the kitchen.

Scobie asked his father, "Do you think it's possible that I could have known?"

Sam shrugged. "Yes, I think it's possible," he said.

Matthew sat on the couch, staring into the fire. Sam found an unfinished airplane model in the closet.

The next morning, they ate a big breakfast—hot cereal and bacon and eggs and coffee. Then Scobie and Matthew and Ken and Sam went down to the beach and climbed into the rowboat.

"We have to believe in something," Sam said. He stood at the bow. The wind lifted his hair, the collar of his coat. Scobie and Matthew looked across the bay at the houses. Their father tipped the urn over the water. It was so cold he was breathing clouds.

Early Sunday Morning

You write?" Susan's father asked.

"Yes."

"What?"

"Stories," Scobie said.

"Stories," Mr. Evans repeated, his slightly protruberant eyes puzzled. "Stories." His eyes swiveled up to the ceiling. "Pornography," he muttered.

"I beg your pardon?"

"Pornography."

"What about it?"

Nodding confidentially, Mr. Evans rose and huffed from the kitchen.

Scobie swallowed. "What was that all about?"

"Nothing," Susan said, smiling across the table. "He's just like that."

"I don't understand."

She stood. "Want some more coffee?"

"No thanks."

Through the kitchen window Scobie could see the late-afternoon sunlight patterned across the Atlantic. In the distance, a lighthouse—a pale white sliver—balanced on the waves.

"Does he think all writing is pornography?"

"Who knows?" Susan said. "He gets all these crazy ideas reading *Newsweek*."

As he considered her reply, Scobie slipped into a moment barely remembered—a sense, more than a vision, of sunlight on a carpet.

"Why did he stop teaching music?" he asked.

"Me."

"You?"

"Children. Money. Teaching music in a small New Hampshire town is hardly lucrative."

"But he plays on weekends?"

"Yes."

"Will he be playing tonight?"

"Probably."

"Let's go hear him."

"Really?"

"Yeah."

"O.K. That would be fun. He'd appreciate it." Susan stood at the sink. Beyond her, through another window, Scobie could see laundry flapping on a clothesline.

"I'll be right back," he said. "I have to change. Then let's go for a walk."

He left the kitchen and walked into the living room. A row of windows stretched along the outside wall, and there was a stone fireplace at the far end of the room. The walls were papered in gray. The furniture was a bizarre collection: an upright piano, a heavy Victorian armchair, a mammoth octagonal table with a glass top, and a gold leatherette couch with faded green cushions scattered over it. The room summed up a casual indifference to material possessions. The Evanses did not own a single beautiful object.

Scobie spied a photograph over the piano. Looking closer, he saw that it was Susan, almost unrecognizable in touched-up pastels.

Upstairs, shivering in his cold room, he yanked off his shirt, washed at the sink by the door, and pulled a clean shirt from his suitcase. In the mirror above the sink, his bearded face was pale. He paused, hairbrush in hand, and let the earlier half memory complete itself: a warm midsummer morning in Paris, waking on the couch of a living room somber with shutters and tapestries, waking to the dry touch of a girl named Alice. Now she was married, a mother. What Scobie remembered no longer existed.

When he went back downstairs, Susan was in her parents' room, sitting in a rocking chair talking to her mother. Eleven-month-old Kathy was asleep in her crib. There were newspapers scattered on the floor, children's clothes piled on the bureau. A crucifix hung on one wall, and from a small table in the corner a radio was broadcasting a Boston talk show.

Mrs. Evans sat on the edge of the bed, folding laundry. She wore a flower-patterned housedress and a blue sweater. Her dark hair was cut short. Her face was long and thin;

not cold but reserved. She said little, merely watched—calculating, Scobie felt; testing him. She looked up with her brown, opaque eyes and smiled cautiously.

"Hello," he said from the doorway. He nodded toward Susan. "Shall we go for our walk?"

She left the rocking chair and joined him in the hallway, where they pulled on their overcoats. "We won't be long, Mom."

The afternoon had become overcast. Shadows of clouds spun across the hard ground. Susan took Scobie's arm and they started down the hill that led to the beach and the boardwalk. Most of the houses they passed were closed for the winter, their loose shutters rattling in the sea breeze. Patches of sand covered the road.

"It's like a ghost town," Scobie said.

"In the summer there are over a hundred thousand people here. Now there's only a few thousand."

"I like it. It's kind of romantic." Scobie struggled to light a cigarette in the wind, gave up.

At the bottom of the hill they turned left onto a narrow sidewalk. They passed a motel with bright pink cabins, a restaurant with a "Closed for the Season" sign on its plate-glass window, and came to the beginning of the seawall. A quarter of a mile away, the beach stretched white and empty.

"I'm sorry my parents are so difficult," Susan said.

"Oh, they're not so difficult."

"They like you," Susan said.

"They do?"

"Yes."

"How can you tell?"

"You make them laugh."

"First your father thinks I'm a Svengali. Now he thinks I write pornography." He stopped. "Here, wait a minute. Face the wind." Using her back as shelter, he lit a cigarette.

Across the street, dozens of motels looked out over the ocean.

"I think my father was here once," Scobie said. "In the forties. He and a girl friend came to dance."

"There's a casino farther on, with a big ballroom. Famous bands used to play there."

"Maybe that's where he went."

"My parents were probably here at the same time," Susan said. "Your father might have walked past them on the boardwalk."

"Or bumped into them dancing. They did dance, didn't they?"

"Yes." She laughed.

When they reached the beach, the only figure in sight was a man in a green parka, moving slowly across the sand, bent over something that looked like a short broom. Seagulls squealed above the surf.

"What's he doing?" Scobie asked.

"Looking for gold. That's a Geiger counter."

"Gold?"

"You know, watches and rings, or coins—stuff people lose on the beach over the summer."

"You're kidding."

"No. Lots of people do it."

"Do they ever find anything?"

"I don't know. I suppose they must."

Scobie looked away to the pale-blue bandstand at the side of the beach. "Is that where your father played?" he asked.

"Yes."

"It must have been fun coming here with him."

"It was," Susan said. "He was my hero—standing up there with his trumpet, the center of attraction. I used to watch him from here, right near those steps."

A Trailways bus hissed around a corner and disappeared.

"Do they know we're living together?" Scobie asked.

"I doubt it."

"They must."

"No, I don't think they do. Not consciously, I mean. They wouldn't be likely to discuss it unless we brought it up."

They approached the old casino—a large, wooden, two-story building wild with balconies and fire escapes. The central roof was domed. The remnants of half a century's posters merged into the worn white walls: a dancer's slipper kicking out into the void, the electric guitar of some briefly illuminated star vanishing in a maze of colored letters.

Scobie turned to face the sea. Whitecaps were breaking along the shore. A single green garbage can leaned in the wind. The man with the Geiger counter met the breakers, straightened, and began a fresh sweep of the beach.

Scobie took Susan's arm and they started walking back toward the house. "Hear the wind?"

"Yes."

"That sound always reminds me of when I was little. A tree went down in our garden during a storm. The whole trunk split and the top came crashing onto the ground."

"When I was little, every time there was a storm my grandmother used to make us all come into her bedroom and she'd sprinkle us with holy water." Susan laughed. "One time she sprinkled us with ink by mistake."

"Isn't it weird to think that while I was watching that tree come down you were here in New Hampshire doing something else at exactly the same time? I wish there were some way of figuring out what we were each doing at exactly the same moment."

When they got back to the house, they found Susan's family eating in the kitchen, sitting on the benches that ran along either side of the table. Mr. Evans was feeding Kathy. Eric and Melissa, who were twelve and thirteen, sat across from him. Mrs. Evans was at the stove. They all looked up when Scobie and Susan entered.

"Where've you been?" Mr. Evans asked, stuffing a pickle into Kathy's mouth.

"Walking," Susan said.

She and Scobie sat down to eat.

"Hey, you know what happened at work yesterday?" Mr. Evans slammed his palm on the table. "Some guys picked my car up and turned it around sideways in the parking lot. Yeah, they did."

The children laughed.

Mr. Evans fed Kathy another pickle. "Well," he said,

counting heads with a flourish. "Here we are. All under one roof. If they got us now, we'd all go together."

Six miles south of the Evanses' house, on the left-hand side of the old highway to Boston, Harry's Night Club sat blinking—a flash of beer signs and arrows in the dark, wooded landscape. Scobie parked his Volkswagen between two decrepit Cadillacs and followed Susan through the front door, a baroque work of padded silver, to a small vestibule, where a redheaded woman in vermilion hot pants took their coats. The club itself was a large room with a bar along one wall. At the sides, Scobie could make out the shapes of tables lit by flickering candles. There was a square wooden dance floor in the middle and, against the far wall, a miniature stage on which sat a drummer, clumsily nonchalant, an owl-eyed accordionist, and Mr. Evans, halfway through the chorus of "That Old Black Magic," his trumpet glistening in the soft light. Another, younger girl in hot pants led Susan and Scobie to a table. They ordered drinks.

Mr. Evans saw them and played a quick riff on his trumpet, shaking his head and smiling. Scobie glanced at Susan. Her large, blue eyes were watching her father.

Mr. Evans consulted the accordionist, shook out his horn, tapped his foot, and led the band into "Hello, Dolly!"

Though it was Saturday night, the club was practically empty. One couple—an old man and a young woman—sat close together at a table in a corner. Two girls in miniskirts and frilly shirts sat at the bar, watching a television

set attached to the wall above the bottles and glasses. The
bartender watched with them, idly rubbing his counter.

After Mr. Evans had roared into the mircrophone a final,
guttural imitation of Louis Armstrong, the musicians put
down their instruments and left the stage. One of the girls
at the bar slid off her stool and twitched over to the jukebox, dropped in a coin, made a selection, and returned to
her place. "Aquarius" filled the room.

Mr. Evans collapsed on a chair next to Susan.

"Hello, Daddy," she said.

He ruffled his hair and peered suspiciously about the
room. "I didn't think you were really coming."

"Of course we were."

"Well, how do you like it?"

"Nice," Susan said.

"Weird," Scobie said.

Mr. Evans sat back in his chair and laughed. "He thinks
it's weird."

"Who runs it?" Scobie asked.

"The Mafia."

"Really?"

Mr. Evans waved to the waitress.

"How do you know?" Scobie asked.

Mr. Evans grimaced conspiratorially.

The drummer and the accordionist came over. "This is
my daughter, Susan," Mr. Evans said. "And her . . . boy
friend, Scobie. Billy and Eddie." Billy was the drummer,
Eddie the accordionist.

Scobie shook hands with them and sat back down.

Mr. Evans ordered a round of drinks.

The second girl had left her stool. She chose "A Rainy Night in Georgia" and went back to the bar.

"Where you from?" Billy asked, rapping his fingers on the edge of the table. His blond hair was cut short and carefully combed, and he wore a green suit that matched his shirt and tie. He held his head as if studying his profile in a mirror.

"Boston," Scobie said.

"What do you do?"

"He's a writer," Mr. Evans said.

"Yeah? That's great, really great. I just read a fantastic book. 'The Plot.' Ever read that? Great book. I'm a prolific reader."

Mr. Evans laughed.

Eddie looked at the empty dance floor. "We're playing the wrong music," he said, and sighed.

"Yep," Mr. Evans said. "Wrong music, wrong place, wrong time."

"You should write a book about us," Mr. Evans said. "We could tell you a few things. Eh, Eddie? Back in the old days we used to play vaudeville." Mr. Evans leaned forward. "Guys used to smoke dope then, too—you know that? Yeah, well, they did. You should sit us all down one night, start us talking, and turn on the tape recorder. That would be some book." Mr. Evans jiggled his knees nervously. "What *do* you write about?" he asked.

"Oh, you know, people."

"Sex?"

"Daddy, Scobie is *not* a pornographer," Susan said.

"Break's over," Eddie said, standing.

The three musicians returned to the stage.

"Request?" Mr. Evans called.

" 'As Time Goes By,' " Scobie said.

"That's not your kind of music."

"We like it," Susan said.

Mr. Evans began the song.

Scobie, leaning back, suddenly noticed that there were 45's tacked onto the ceiling—hundreds of records, the refuse, presumably, of many jukeboxes. He was about to point them out to Susan when an elfin old man with a whiskey bottle in his hip pocket slid onto the dance floor and started floating in the arms of an invisible lover.

"Scobie, I'm tired." Susan's cheek touched his as she spoke in his ear.

"Will your father be hurt?"

"No, he'll understand. It's late."

They walked to the bar, paid the waitress, and turned to wave goodbye to Mr. Evans—but his eyes were closed above his trumpet.

It was cold outside, the air threatening snow. Scobie's nostrils tingled as he started the Volkswagen. He pulled out onto the highway, his headlights briefly catching a red-eyed squirrel, and quickly moved the car into fourth gear. On the radio a barely audible Otis Redding was singing "The Dock of the Bay." They passed a few gas stations, a church, a ghostly shopping center. The heater slowly warmed the car. Scobie opened the glove compartment and handed Susan a small tin box. She lit a joint, inhaled, and handed it to Scobie. They drove in silence until they reached the boulevard in front of the casino. Susan rolled down her window and breathed deeply. The smell of salty air rushed through the car. Scobie could hear the waves breaking on the beach. He lit a cigarette.

The house was dark. Susan took the key from her purse and opened the front door. A cat jumped off a chair and scurried into the living room.

"Do you want some tea?" Susan whispered.

"Yes."

They closed the kitchen door behind them.

"Your parents are very strange," Scobie said.

"I wish we could sleep together tonight."

"Me, too."

"It's hard, having children, don't you think?" Susan asked. "They're bound to break your heart in some way."

The water boiled and Susan poured tea. The hot, sweet liquid immediately made Scobie sleepy.

"The hardest thing must be realizing they've grown up," Susan said.

"Who?"

"Children. I mean, there comes a time when parents must realize that you are what they were when they had you years and years ago. If you see what I mean?"

"I do."

Susan yawned. "Let's go to bed."

They emptied their cups in the sink, turned off the light, and climbed the stairs. In the hallway they kissed.

"Good night," Scobie said.

"Good night," she whispered.

Scobie undressed quickly and got under the covers— three blankets and Susan's old Girl Scout sleeping bag.

Waves were rolling mysteriously in the darkness beyond his window.

When he was little, he remembered, he used to go to bed early and lie awake listening to the swish of car wheels and the whine of speeding sirens on the street below, the shrill voices of other children playing kickball on the sidewalk, the breaking of bottles in the alley out back. And he remembered a night before Christmas when the door suddenly opened and the figure of his father—the shape, motion, smell of his father—had stepped across the room, climbed into his bed, and lay there with him listening.

"Do you hear?" his father had asked.

"What?"

"Footsteps, I think. Do you hear?"

A delicate touch, a rap on the rooftop . . .

"What?"

"Reindeer," his father had said.

Scobie awoke Sunday morning to the sound of voices arguing in the hallway. He recognized Mr. Evans' voice, then, sliding in with supplication, Mrs. Evans' voice, and then—angry, tearful—Susan's voice. He could not understand what they were saying. A door slammed, there was a moment's silence, and the argument resumed, this time in one of the other bedrooms. The muffled voices seemed part of his dreams.

Footsteps descended the stairs. Another door slammed.

Scobie pulled on his blue jeans and shirt, brushed his teeth, and was lacing up his boots when the door to his room quietly opened. It was Susan.

Her face, still soft with sleep, looked like her face in the photograph downstairs: alarmed and vulnerable. She had been crying, which only made her large blue eyes seem larger.

"What's the matter?" he asked.

She sat down next to him on the bed. "It's so silly," she said.

"What were you arguing about?"

"Church."

"What about it?"

"They wanted me to go."

"You're kidding."

"No." She rubbed her eyes.

"What happened?"

"Oh, they came up pretending they wanted to put the sewing machine in my room. Then they asked me if I was going with them. When I said no they started to argue, and Daddy started to cry, and Mom wanted to know what she was supposed to tell the children."

"Do they think you still go to church?" Scobie asked. "Haven't you been here before and not gone?"

"Well . . . no. It was always too much of a hassle," she said. "I went to make them happy."

"That's incredible." Scobie finished lacing his boots and rose. "Are they at church now?"

"Yes."

"Then let's have a nice, quiet breakfast."

In the kitchen, they made coffee and eggs and sat down to eat. When they had finished, Scobie said, "It's eleven o'clock. Let's leave in an hour."

"Yes."

"Susan, for Godsake, don't worry. It's not your fault. They have to learn you're a little different from them."

"They think it's all because of you."

"*Me?*"

"They think you've influenced me in some terrible way." She laughed. "Svengali that you are."

"That's ridiculous. You should just tell them what you think."

"I did, but they wouldn't listen. Daddy started crying."

"Well, don't worry about it. If they really love you, they'll stop bothering you sooner or later."

"I'm not sure about that."

"Look at it this way. You aren't going to change, right? *They've* got to change."

"They can't."

"They've got to."

"Oh, Scobie, you don't understand. They really *believe* these things."

"I understand that they can't expect you to believe what they believe."

"But they do."

"They shouldn't."

"Scobie, let's go." Susan pressed her small hands against her cheeks.

"You're the one who wanted to come," he said.

"I want to go."

"O.K."

Scobie was upstairs packing his suitcase when Susan's family returned from church. The children were noisy—

changing clothes, banging the piano, opening and closing the refrigerator—but Scobie could sense behind the racket the melancholy silence of Mr. and Mrs. Evans.

"Scobie?" Susan was waiting for him in the hallway.

"Coming." He picked up his suitcase and joined her.

Susan's parents were alone in the kitchen, Mr. Evans reading the Sunday *Globe*, Mrs. Evans peeling potatoes by the sink. Mr. Evans was wearing an old flannel shirt, slightly elevated by his stomach, and a canvas captain's cap. Around his neck hung a pair of binoculars. He didn't look up.

"Are you going?" Mrs. Evans asked.

"Yes," Scobie said. "I want to avoid the Sunday rush."

For the first time that weekend, Mrs. Evans gave him an open stare. Then she glanced out the window and said, "Weather's clear."

"Yes," Scobie said.

"Goodbye, Mom. Thanks for everything." Susan looked down at the silent figure hunched above the newspaper. "Goodbye, Daddy."

"Goodbye, Mr. Evans," Scobie said hurriedly. "Goodbye, Mrs. Evans."

He picked up the two suitcases and carried them out to the car. He could see his breath as he dropped them into the back seat. He unlocked the door for Susan and started the motor. The windshield misted. He wiped it clear with his hand. "All set?"

Susan nodded and he backed the car out of the driveway. When he looked through the front window again, he saw Mr. Evans standing on the steps of the house.

Susan rolled down her window and waved, and her father, clutching his binoculars, called out, "When're you coming back?"

"Easter," Susan said.

A smile struggled against his sternness and was gone. Slowly, insouciantly, he waved, then disappeared back into the house.

Scobie and Susan drove down the small hill, past the summer cottages, then along the beach, past the motels and restaurants and the casino. They drove past the liquor stores and supermarkets and parking lots and drive-ins until they reached the highway, where they turned south and headed for Boston.

Jewels and Binoculars

QUENTIN knew from his compulsory geology classes that he was walking across what used to be a glacial island. Now it was a small New England college town. All that was left of the glacier was a river stretching from Canada to New York. Last fall, he had stood on the bank of that river, along with forty-seven other sophomore geology students, and stared at several preserved dinosaur tracks and thought that his consciousness should have included memories of a father dinosaur leading his family away from the approaching glacier and into the desert to die. But his mind could rarely move beyond the short history of the town: the Indians, the pioneers, the long winters, the college, the new highway stretching as far as the river and ringed with Howard Johnsons and supermarkets. Even the Indians sometimes seemed too mystical to be real.

Quentin's roommate, Larry, walked at his side. It was a warm May evening. Music floated down from open fra-

ternity windows. They climbed a grassy hill to the quad
where students in tie-dyed T-shirts were playing touch
football. Sunlight fell through the trees in golden circles.
A flag on top of the distant chapel curled slowly. A blue
Frisbee was caught in a branch of one of the trees. Quentin
thought of his father standing on a terrace with a drink
in his hand, turning and smiling as he pushed his glasses
back up his nose. Larry led the way along the edge of the
quad to the war memorial. On the playing fields below, a
baseball game was in progress; small figures crouched and
ran.

"I used to play baseball," Larry said.

"You did?"

"Yeah. Shortstop."

They read the names on the memorial:

> PETER TAYLOR, '16, THE MARNE
> GEORGE MASON, '40, SICILY
> OSCAR LEVANTHAL, '42, NORMANDY

"Do you realize how strange it'll be to come back here
in twenty years and see that baseball game still going on?"
Larry asked.

"Yes." Quentin felt the presence of all the former students who had stood here—serious young men in wide
white flannels and tight sleeveless sweaters.

"Let's go to the bird sanctuary," Larry said.

As they ran down the hill, Quentin remembered looking
for gooseberries in Italy with his brothers. They had found
a Second World War bunker buried in the woods. What

was the name of the town? Bocca something. He tried to remember. Bocca. Bocca. "Bocca di Magra," he said aloud when they reached the fields.

"What?"

"Bocca di Magra. That's where we stayed in Italy one summer."

"I went to Italy once," Larry said, looking ahead at the treeline. "With my folks. Rome and Florence, that's all we saw. Museums, museums, museums."

They walked slowly across the soccer fields, past the baseball diamond and tennis courts, to a small path that led them into the woods. A hazy light filtered through the leaves. Most of the trees were pines, evenly spaced, like statues. The ground was covered with soft, damp pine needles. Birds sang in the trees.

"It sounds like they're talking," Larry said.

"Maybe they are."

"Listen."

"It's like stepping into a music box," Quentin whispered.

"I wonder who decided this should be a bird sanctuary?"

"I don't know. A good man, though, whoever he was."

"I wish I knew more about birds," Larry said. "I wish I knew their names. I don't know anything about nature."

"Me, either."

"I mean, what kind of flower is that?"

"I don't know," Quentin said.

They reached a small clearing and lay down. Pine needles surrounded them like the sea. The light was dimming. Quentin could hear nothing but the birds and his own breathing and his beating heart. His hands lay folded on his chest. The clouds had turned red. When he moved his head to the left or right, the view stayed with him, superimposing itself over the new view: treetops, Larry's face, treetops.

"What was Bocca di what'sis like?" Larry asked.

"I was pretty young," Quentin said. "I can't remember too much. We rented a white cottage on the side of a hill. It had green shutters, I think. I could see the water from my bedroom window. There was a beach. And a jukebox that was always playing Paul Anka. My brother collected plastic spoons."

"Spoons?"

"You know, ice-cream spoons. They were bright colors —made of plastic. He must have had hundreds of them by the end of the summer."

"Which brother?" Larry asked.

"Scobie. The oldest."

They lay and listened to the birds. An airplane droned overhead.

"It'll be dark soon," Larry said.

"I know."

"Want to go to Deke?"

"Sure. Why not?"

They laughed quietly. Quentin heard his laughter free itself from his throat and rise to the sky. The treetops were fluttering like leafy wings. He brought his hands up and covered his eyes. He could smell his fingers and remembered lying by the side of a swimming pool and smelling chlorine on these same fingers. No, not the same fingers.

Different fingers. Cells had died, new cells had been born. His whole body was different. Yet something in him was unchanging, something seemed to stretch back to birth; his body shed layers of skin like a snake, but something inside his head remained permanent enough to observe even its own coming death.

He rolled over onto his stomach. A fresh, cool breeze brushed his face, and he shivered.

"Let's sleep here some night," Larry said.

"O.K."

"Do you have a sleeping bag?"

"Yeah," Quentin said.

Under the trees, shadows and objects merged. Quentin listened to his heart beating up through the earth. The sound of laughter reached him, disappeared. He heard car wheels on gravel, the ring of a bicycle bell. He felt as if he were staring through curtains. The birds were suddenly quiet—someone had shut the music box. He could not understand why, a chemical himself, he did not simply become a blade of grass, or a tree. "It's so beautiful," he said.

"What?"

"Beautiful."

"Oh, yeah."

"I think we should sleep out tonight."

"We'll never get it together," Larry said.

"We should try."

"Quentin?"

"Yeah?"

"We have a visitor."

Quentin sat up and looked.

At the edge of the clearing, almost invisible in the dim light, was a white dog. He took a step forward, very slowly straightened his back and stiffened, his right paw suspended. He was stalking. He began to move again, slowly lifting his front legs high with each step, his nose stretched ahead like a pointing finger. He crossed the clearing and disappeared into the woods on the other side. Once, he turned and grinned at Quentin. Then he was gone.

"I'm cold," Larry said.

"Let's go."

They stood and brushed pine needles from their jeans

"You know what my brother's girl friend said the universe was?" Quentin asked, looking up at the first stars. " 'A complex network of imaginations.' "

The path was dark. Larry led the way, groping for trees. Walking on the pine needles, Quentin felt as if he were wearing slippers, and he remembered Christmas at his grandmother's house, the blue snowlight on the ceiling.

The path ended, and he followed Larry onto the field. "Full moon," he said.

The tennis courts looked like swimming pools.

"That's pretty nice," Larry said, as they climbed the hillside.

"What?"

"What your brother's girl friend said."

"Oh, yeah. She's an amazing chick. You'd like her."

Quentin lay on a bed in George's room and watched Marty's worried, sloping forehead gleaming as he hovered above the record player and dropped some albums into place. He moved his hands cautiously, deliberately, as if performing a delicate operation. He'll be a doctor, Quentin thought. A candle shimmered, Indians danced on the curtains. On the other side of the room, George sat next to Larry on a sagging couch, his large, thin, freckled hands resting on his knees. Marty sat back down on a cushion on the floor, and The Grateful Dead sang through the two huge speakers in opposite corners of the room. Quentin, listening, imagined long shady streets, lawns, hedges, slow lavender sunsets, whirring sprinklers, highways reaching out to California, drugstores, drive-ins, girls in hair curlers, and empty American towns at three in the morning. The images flicked through his head like postcards. He felt as if his life lay trapped in its own past, a caged extinction. This room, his friends, the college—they eluded him. He wanted to touch Larry, he wanted to make sure he was really there. The music spoke to him of an incoherent history, an imitation mythology. He and Larry, unlike the Indians on the curtains, were dancing an unremembered dance, peeling back film upon film of consciousness only to discover that what they valued was not theirs but someone else's—the black man's, perhaps, or the Jew's, the renegade American's dream of starting over again. Quentin stared up at the swirls of light on the ceiling. They reminded him of sunspots, reflections from the sea, some childhood sensation. He flexed his fingers and sat up. The bed rolled beneath him like a wave. Larry was peering between his knees at the carpet, tapping his toe to the music. "Let's see what's happening downstairs," Quentin said.

"O.K."

"Bring the cigarettes," Marty said.

The four of them walked down to the first floor of the fraternity, then through another door and down to the long, dark bar in the basement. The room stank of stale beer. There was a jukebox against the far wall, a glowing red machine that reduced the voices in the room to a soothing electric murmur. Boys and girls were crowded around the beer keg. Many of them were drunk and laughed with their mouths wide open and their heads thrown back. Quentin, Larry, George, and Marty moved through the bar and along a corridor, past the furnace, to the "goat-room"—a small, round room with a domed ceiling where in the old days initiation rites had been held. There were three descending tiers of wooden seats around the walls. The room was dense with cigarette smoke. A band was playing on the floor, surrounded by speakers and amplifiers.

Quentin and Larry squatted together and watched the band, like two bushmen watching the sunset.

"I need some coffee," Larry whispered.

"I'm hungry."

"Marty, you hungry?" Larry asked.

"Yeah, sure."

"George?"

"O.K."

"Marty, you drive," Quentin said.

"You must be kidding."

"No, man, you drive."

"What's a steering wheel?"

"Oh, come on."

"I'll drive," George said.

They went out through a basement door. The air was suddenly cold and clear. They all stood in the moonlight and inhaled loudly.

"O.K., George, you're in charge," Quentin said.

"Don't worry about a thing," George said. "Now, let's see. Key. We need the key."

"Here." Marty handed him a ring of keys. "The one with the square top."

They climbed into Marty's Saab. George turned the key and revved the engine.

"Seat belts?"

"Check," Larry said.

"Lights?"

"Here. O.K. Lights."

"Let's see. I guess that's it."

"Emergency brake?" Quentin asked.

"Oh, yeah." George released the brake. "All right. Here we go."

They left the fraternity parking lot and turned onto the road.

"Where're we going?" George asked.

"Dunkin' Donuts."

The night sped by outside the car window, the two-mile journey taking but a few minutes, the landscape revolving around them like a repetitious movie background, an endless string of neon lights: McDonalds, Hardees, an Esso station, a miniature golf course frozen in violet light.

Behind the pink, S-shaped counter of Dunkin' Donuts stood a girl in a pink uniform. She smiled as they came in. A middle-aged man in a plaid shirt sat at the end of the counter, chewing. They sat down on the pink stools.

"What'll it be?" the girl asked, pointing up to a pink menu on the wall.

"Uh, yeah, four coffees," George said.

"Black or white?"

"Oh, yeah, uh, black."

"Four blacks?"

"Uh, yeah, I guess so."

The girl laughed and shook her head. She had red hair and blue eyes and a wide smile.

"And four doughnuts," Quentin said.

"What kind?"

"Cinnamon."

"Chocolate," Larry said.

"One of each," Quentin said.

"O.K." She laughed. She left them and walked to the doughnut rack.

"She is the most beautiful girl I have ever seen," Quentin whispered to Larry.

"She is indeed beautiful."

"Larry, I'm in love."

"She is very beautiful," Marty whispered. "Very, very beautiful."

"Here you go," she said, setting down the coffee and the doughnuts.

Quentin looked at the pink name tag on her dress.

"Lilly."

"Yes?" She smiled.

"Why is everything in here pink?"

"I don't know."

"Lilly is a beautiful name," Quentin said.

She blushed. "Thank you."

Another customer came in and she left to serve him.

"I'm in *love*," Quentin whispered.

The pinkness around him made him blink. It was blinding. He watched Lilly work efficiently behind the counter. Her hands were wrinkled and calm. Two policemen came in for a cup of coffee and Quentin couldn't keep his eyes open. "Hi, boys," they said. They talked to Lilly and made her laugh, and when they left they said, "Drive careful, boys." Larry played the jukebox. The man in the plaid shirt paid and left, still chewing. Lilly danced behind the counter.

"What time is it?" George asked.

"Three-thirty."

"I have a four-o'clock curfew," he said, standing.

"Why?"

"I want to get up tomorrow."

"Good night, Lilly," Quentin said.

"Good night." She smiled. "No, don't."

Larry looked down at the money in his hand and then back up at her. "No?"

"Forget it," she said. "No one will ever know."

"Far out," Quentin said. "Far fucking out."

"Good night," she called after them.

They drove back to the college over a highway as empty as an undiscovered river. Quentin, sitting in the back seat, felt exhausted, bodiless, momentarily at peace with the thought that the earth was no longer a place to be explored, that

dwelling on a lost world was a kind of sophisticated senti-
mentality that would never move him into time, into the
fabric of things, into a flow that contained more than his
own existence. Perhaps, he thought, staring through the
car window, life is indeed a dream, and only those who
demand a sense of reality are left unfulfilled. In the half
dark he looked at his hands, marveling that they had once
clutched the watery insides of his mother's stomach.

"Let us off at the corner," Larry said.

George stopped the car. Larry and Quentin got out.
They said good night and slammed the door shut. The
Saab drove slowly up the street. Quentin could see the
tail lights turning into the parking lot. The traffic signal
hanging over the intersection blinked on and off. He and
Larry crossed the street in silence and sat down on the
dew-covered common.

"You tired?" Larry asked.

"Yeah."

A car turned the corner and vanished along the road.

"Let's race," Quentin said.

"Race?"

"Yeah."

"Where?" Larry asked.

"Across the common."

"Don't be absurd." Larry laughed.

"Come on." Quentin stood. "It'll be good for you."

"No."

"Come on."

"You're crazy," Larry said, still laughing.

"Come on, come on."

"Absolutely crazy."

"Ready?" Quentin asked.

"Wait a minute, wait a minute."

They both crouched down in starting positions.

"I just want you to remember that I was a baseball star and can run like the wind," Larry said.

"On your mark—"

"I have the speed of a tornado, my friend."

"Get set, *go*."

Quentin pushed up and started running as fast as he could. Larry was right at his side. Quentin could hear only their footsteps and their panting. It seemed to him that they were running straight into the moon. His lungs ached and his legs felt like water, but he made himself run even faster, on across the white common, on toward the shimmering dinosaur he now saw leading his family away from the approaching glacier and into the desert to die.

Balcony

I AM on Crete, watching the moon beyond the balcony. Susan sits inside, on the bed, embroidering a peacock on one of my shirts. If I lean back I can just see her hands pulling the brightly colored yarn back and forth. She has the body of a dancer: tall, thin, small-breasted, vaguely graceful. She dances slowly, casually, her eyes lowered. The music in Yorgo's discotheque muffles the voices around me and slaps against the back of my brain like surf. I remember sitting on a train, in a compartment with a girl and an old woman. The girl shifts her weight and turns her hands over in the dim light. The old lady is asleep, her mouth open in a small circle. I stare at the point where the girl's blue jeans pinch in below her belly, bunch, and spread out over her hips. Our eyes meet. She smiles. The old lady tilts toward the window, snoring. The girl leans forward and I kiss her. Walking back to our room, Susan and I stop to watch the black waves, laced with luminescent white, roar into the water-front. The crumbling Turkish minaret is poised above us in the moonlight like an ancient rocket ship. I look at Susan's face in the silver light and feel suddenly empty, horrified at the strangeness of what I see. She smiles and I kiss her. But I can't get the image, Susan's distance, out of my mind. She is lying in bed, her hair covering her shoulders. Her mouth is wide and her eyes pale-blue. Her hands are small, and when we make love they flutter along my back like butterflies. Her fingers are thick with rings. Gold, silver, copper, turquoise, and amber sparkle as she speaks. I am trying to get close to her. The whitewashed houses of Crete, clustered together at the edge of the sea, remind me of pueblo homes. Details shimmer into view: pomegranate and lemon trees in the fields, donkeys climbing the hazy hillsides, blue-green waves rustling the bleached pebbles. Above the main square of this town hangs a fifteen-foot neon sign of a phoenix in flames. At night, a lunatic prowls the narrow streets, a huge, shuffling adolescent who calls out the names of imaginary lovers as he looms through the moonlight.

"Scobie, did I ever tell you I was once a majorette?"

"What?"

Susan laughs. "It's true."

"When?"

"High school. I hated it. I only did it so I culd get into college."

When Susan speaks, she sometimes lifts her hands, as if she expects rain or gold to fall from the ceiling, then lets them settle like doves onto her lap. I am meeting her in the cool spring evening and we are walking through the shadows of trees. She wears a short dress and a corduroy jacket. Kissing her while I'm still asleep, I think she is a man, and the unexpected touch of a man's cool lips thrills me. But when I reach down and discover only her mysterious female moistness, I awake, remembering who I am and what I am imagining. She sighs and clasps her hands to my shoulders, gentleness and lust mingling strangely in a smile, her head thrust back and her fingers brushing my cheeks like feathers. I hear a whisper raging in my blood, commanding me: "Vanish, *vanish.*" Sex, like speech, separates form from matter, and to think of myself as the merging of the two is as futile as trying to disappear in Susan's arms. There is always a struggle. I am trying to understand her, to know her, but the words I use have a life of their own, they won't represent what's really there. The girl's mouth opens wide. I touch the side of her cheek. We both rise and walk quietly into the corridor of the clicking, speeding train. Her fingers probe, plunge down over my belt. I feel the small of my back snap, my body double as she grunts and collapses against my chest. She straightens, smiles, and returns unsteadily to the compartment. I step across to the bathroom door, open it, lock it behind me, pull off my bluejeans and underpants, and pry open the cracked bathroom window. Cold night air hits my face, and for one brief instant before throwing out my underpants I see moonlight on the tracks. My face, so vague it could be expectation, hovers in the tarnished depths of the mirror behind the bar. All around me the shapes of dancers uncoil and sing, "She blew my nose and then she blew my mind!" Next to my face, equally obscure, is Susan's. They both smile.

"Do you think I'm beautiful?"

"Yes."

"Really?"

"Really."

"Sometimes I don't feel very beautiful," she says, curling up with her head on my shoulder.

Leafy trees line the waterfront. Motorbikes sputter up and down the main street. Children, walking home from school in their neat blue uniforms, shyly eye the foreigners on their way to Israel or India who live in orange tents on the beach and dance in Yorgo's discotheque. Fishermen bring in their catch at the end of the day and a small crowd gathers to watch them unload, young Greek men standing with their arms around each other's shoulders. In the *kafenions,* old men in baggy, frayed flannels and dark blue sweaters play cards and sip sweet black coffee. The environment entertains us, speech is an entertainment, separate and abstract—no longer the necessary element, the strange and loving force once spoken to fill a silence. A heart-shaped pool of sweat has gathered on Susan's back. She wriggles her wrists, a ripple of bracelets. Behind her is the sea. I can smell it: the tangy scent of adventure and lost love. Through the window I can see across the flat, white rooftops to the minaret and the mountains beyond. A faint echo of sadness fills the air. It seems that silent armies rise from the rocks to watch. The stones look like ancient helmets. I can almost feel the blades of broken swords beneath my feet. Under the soil lie the ruins of civilization: bone, gold, marble. But I can imagine no people, no paintings, no language. Only an empty, disintegrating monolith—Knossos destroyed by an earthquake from

Atlantis. Lizards glitter in the sunlight. Cicadas purr. Susan stumbles and I catch her. I have never felt such a soothing absence of tension with a woman before. Our love is almost unquestionable, a vibration in the air accepted as naturally as the air itself. She searches the landscape for every instance of beauty, curious as a child at the edge of the ocean. Sunlight reveals soft, swirling down at the back of her neck, checkers her profile with delicate shadows, glazes her fingertips. I look out the window at the brown hillsides, the olive trees, the winding road, the motionless clouds. I have reduced my beliefs to a simple faith in song, or sunlight, or stone. The dancers buckle under some sudden weight, then fly high with sudden freedom. They form a single, quivering shadow that changes shape as if the discotheque's lights were flickering in a wind. Turning away from the window, I look at Susan's half-hidden face. She is asleep, her hands pressed to her chin, her fingers touching her lips. Thoughts, or dreams, wrinkle her eyelids.

"Susan."

Her eyes tremble, open in confusion. I sit down on the bed with two cups of tea.

"Sleep well?"

"Very." She smiles. "I dreamed you wrote a white book. Everything was white. The cover, the pages, the print."

So we have come here together to escape the habits of comprehension. She smells of sleep. Darkness presses at the window. Cats shiver over walls, and by the bus station children from the mountain villages wait for their buses to take them home. I can almost imagine the ride: the headlights on the weaving road, the sudden sleepiness, the cold, thin air rushing in the windows. Susan laughs and touches her breasts, as if plotting some lovely revelation. I am so tired of irony. I meet Susan dancing. She comes from a small town in New Hampshire, I have grown up all over the world, yet we both love the same things, the same illusive moments that have nothing to do with history but which we tend to categorize mnemonically. Her face, her gestures and habits, even her dreams now seem familiar to me. Sometimes I'm bored, as I'm sure she must be. Sometimes I masturbate, my own hands uniquely erotic, and sometimes I sleep with other women. But usually the familiarity attracts me back to Susan, holds me to her, makes me want always to have this other person as close to me as myself. Christmas is coming. I can feel it in the quick north wind. Since I am tempted to view life as if it were already painted or written by an invisible hand, I come to Crete to look at things with a fresh eye. I am only twenty-five years old. I want to cross the distances between people, between Susan and myself. I want to avoid barriers, lines, edges, borders. We meet Pat in the discotheque. The wind whines along the telephone wires as we climb into the mountains and sit with him in his cave. He pulls a large, black square of hashish from a pouch and holds it above one of the lamps, turning it over and over, then crumbling a piece into his pipe. The pipe is inlaid with silver and some kind of blue stone.

"I lived on a houseboat in India," he says, smiling, his beard shaking, then settling. "Way out in the country, man. I was all alone. In the morning I'd jump over the side and swim against the current. The current was so strong I didn't move. I stayed right by the side of the boat. I swam until I was tired, then got back in the boat and made some tea and smoked a while. And every winter I'd hitch to Scotland and work on the ski slopes. In the spring I'd hitch back to India."

Susan's arm absently brushes mine. Her touch amazes me, the way laughter amazes a baby. I think I have an image of my parents in my head—an image of deep, intelligent love growing with time—and I think this image makes me want Susan more than sex makes me want strangers. But I realize that I don't know her. I want to, but I don't know how. I have only fantasies to guide me, memories of imagined women, or real women, the ones I kiss or fondle or sleep with or dream about when I comb my hair back and hope I am handsome—all of them so remote that I feel, sitting here trying to remember them, that they are books I once read, and I wish I could remember the titles. I look past Susan's face and into the dark room throbbing with dancers. I try to imagine her twirling a baton and flashing her slim, white thighs beneath the night lights of some high-school football stadium. In front of the cinema a crowd waits for the movie to begin. I can't describe Susan well enough to break down the description and touch the real thing beyond. The *taverna* windows are opaque with steam. Out on the water a green buoy light is blinking on and off. I sit watching the world in the streets below.

"Do you see the woman's face?" Susan asks.

"Where?"

"There, to the left of that farmhouse, down a little. Do

you see? She has eyes, and a beautiful long nose, and a mouth. She's looking up at the sky."

The serene face is formed by the curves of a mountain range. The sun carves shadows in the rocks: her eyes, her hair, her thin brown lips. All past love is sad love; that's what makes it powerful. It's the only other love I know, and it keeps me from knowing Susan because the power I seek in her is also a sadness, a loss, a comfortable, blinding melancholy, as if, somewhere in my head, she were already dead. We travel in magic circles, orbits designed to keep us from the source of what we circle. I live behind my eyes, like a cat. We lead such crazy lives, locked inside our heads. Bottles gleam behind the bar, in front of the mirror. The dance floor is crowded and dense with cigarette smoke. Occasional features, a face or a hand, pulse into view, then quickly disappear. The music drums into me, a wordless chant. Listening seems an act of anarchy, and when the song ends, when the music suddenly drops away, I feel like a betrayed partisan standing on the outskirts of a revolution. We all grow up thinking we are movie stars, that the world is recording our presence. I don't know why. People should speak only to solve a problem. I want to live fully. I want to penetrate the objects around me. The energy of a search might make words mean something again. A new song ebbs into the discotheque. Susan sits motionless as a statue, her face as soft and radiant as marble. One of the dancers separates himself from the shadow and lifts another dancer into the air, a smile on his briefly illuminated face. An old Greek woman, toothless and merry, pokes her head through the

front door, stares curiously, and disappears. Again and
again the scene repeats itself, as if I were changing channels
on a television set. I am trying to get through the world
that fills my mind. I am trying to get close to Susan. I can
hear her fingers flicking the yarn as she fashions the peacock on my shirt. I would like to rise and approach her,
a changed man. I would like to say, I know what I love.
But I would be lying. And the moon is so lovely, hanging
in the black sky above me, perfect, homeless.

Old Friends

Just after dawn, the train stopped at a small station in northern Yugoslavia—a drab, yellow stretch of stone framed by brittle trees and yellow fields. Scobie left the compartment and hurried into the large, high-ceilinged waiting room, where he was served sweet, milky coffee in a plastic cup, and then he walked down the platform outside, breathing clouds of steam and slapping his hands together for warmth. The sun rose in streaks over the fields. Men in high leather boots, thick surplus overcoats, and Russian fur caps moved slowly from doorway to doorway, pushing carts or consulting clipboards. The train, windows blank, hissed. A few other passengers disembarked and ran into the waiting room. Birds fluttered into holes in the station wall. Gradually the sky cleared, becoming open and blue. Scobie reached the end of the platform, lit a cigarette, turned, and walked back along the cold concrete, stamping his feet, trying to shake the sleep from his legs. In the yard of a stone house next to the station he saw an old woman, dressed in black, throwing a bucket of soapy water out onto the hard soil. Her face seemed much too young for her body, but before he could look closer she had disappeared into the house, shutting the door behind her. Scobie continued along the platform, stamping, huffing, thinking of all the trains he had ever been on, all the sights he had seen. He remembered a playground on Long Island, a farmhouse in England, a pasture of sheep in Switzerland. The images—single, isolated—always suggested stories he tried to imagine, lives and worlds through which he passed as quickly and mysteriously as they passed him.

He threw away his cigarette, breathed deeply, held his breath, beat his arms, ran in place, exhaled.

The still, flat sunlight on the platform was crossed by the shadow of a bird. Somewhere over the fields a bell rang, three slow times, and was silent. A man's cough carried through an open window. Plates and voices rattled together inside the station. The train hissed again. Steam rose from the wheels. Metal clanked.

Pacing, Scobie stared at the wagons-lits. The long green carriages had little left of their original elegance. The train was no longer an instrument of romance. Times had changed. Single compartments had been made into double compartments. The dining car didn't exist. The carpets were economically gray, the walls functionally plastic. He couldn't help missing the luxury he had never known—the privilege of sweeping across Europe in the warm, lamp-lit twinkle of the old train. His grandmother and grandfather had visited Europe in the mid-twenties, and he remembered tales of steamer trunks and silk dresses. His father, too, as a boy, had seen Europe, but Scobie could not remember where he had gone or how he had traveled. Life must have been very different then: culture comfortable, songs lighthearted—even the sad ones—and plays gay, even the serious ones. His father had once told him at dinner, exasperated by argument, that people of his own generation had never asked themselves *why* they were doing something; they had just done it, and if they didn't like it they had done something else. *"Some* people of your generation asked themselves why," Scobie had replied, and his father, glumly returning to his meal, had said no more.

Scobie opened the door to the waiting room.

A dozen fellow passengers stood huddled together, drinking coffee and smoking cigarettes. Scobie paid for another cup and went to the window, where he saw his brother crossing the platform. Matthew entered the room and walked to the counter—his eyes still puffy and small from sleep, his reddish blond hair prickly with static, his clothes disorganized.

When Matthew turned, the hot plastic cup burning his hand, and saw Scobie standing like a refugee in his full-length, secondhand overcoat, he almost laughed. Broad, stooped, Scobie's figure demanded unattainable order. His narrow eyes were dry with sleep, and his long hair curled around his ears like feathers.

"Good morning."

"Morning." Scobie stamped his feet. "Christ, it's cold. We'll die in Venice—to coin a phrase."

"It might be warmer, being by the sea."

"I hope so."

Matthew squinted through the window at the train, shining in the sun. When he woke, he had been dreaming of Alexandria, Virginia, of their green brick row house, of the tangled garden out back, of the walk he and Scobie used to take to school across the railroad tracks and past the squat, three-story apartment buildings.

"Do you think Mom and Dad are there yet?" Scobie asked.

"Sure. Quentin's probably there, too. He was supposed to get in last night."

"I worry about him."

"Oh, yeah."

"He smokes too much dope."

"It's the way he smokes it. He makes it into such a big thing."

"He's only eighteen," Scobie said.

"But we weren't like that when we were eighteen."

"Sure we were."

"No, we weren't. We thought it was great, but we *did* things. We got high and went for walks, we got high and went to the movies, we got high and talked. We had fun. We didn't just sit around smoking our brains out in a dark room."

"Matthew, you've become a reactionary."

Matthew put his empty cup down on a table and rubbed his hands together.

Suddenly a whistle blew, doors slammed, and the waiting room emptied. Matthew followed Scobie outside and climbed aboard the train.

The beds of their compartment had been made and folded back to form two facing seats. Franny, Matthew's girl friend, was reading. Susan sat opposite her, a crossword puzzle on her lap.

The train jerked forward a few feet and stopped.

"We're there!" Scobie cried.

They sat and waited, the sun streaming through the window and filling the compartment with swirling motes. Matthew, leaning his head on Franny's shoulder, settled back, half asleep, and felt the sun on his hands, heard voices speaking Greek in the corridor, smelled the dusty fragrance of the faded seats. He thought of Alexandria again, the room he had shared at the top of the house with Scobie—an attic room with a sloping ceiling and beautiful beds: ship's beds with an enclosing rim of wood above the mattresses. His father had made those beds, as well as the bookshelves and the desks that doubled as bureaus. On winter mornings, when the walls were pale blue with the light of reflected snow, that room had smelled much like this train: musty, clothlike.

"Name a poem by Byron," Susan said.

"Which poem?" Scobie asked.

"Any poem."

"Oh, for Chrissake, Susan."

"Then who killed Medusa?"

"Perseus," Franny said.

"Thank you."

Slowly, the train began to move, curving into hilly

country and gathering speed until the trees became quick, snapping sticks spinning past the window. Matthew, pressed against the glass, could see the small station vanishing in the distance, motionless in its rectangle of sunlight. A few figures were moving about on the platform. A dog jumped into the yard of a nearby stone house. The glittering fields revolved out to a perfectly blue sky.

Quentin saw them coming from the *pensione* window, four stumbling shapes in winter coats. Behind them rose a bright-red Ferris wheel, and the yellow and pink houses stretched along the Grand Canal, and the dome of St. Mark's. He opened the window and called, "Hello!" They saw him and waved. His hand, as it fell back to the sill, was as heavy as granite. The afternoon sunlight shimmered on the blue-green water. Passing boats crisscrossed the glow with the webbing of their masts and smokestacks. Twisting to the left, Quentin watched his brothers turn into the door of the *pensione*. Scobie was laughing, bumping into Matthew, pretending to stagger. Watching, Quentin felt small again—the youngest son, the child. He left his room and walked down the corridor to the door of his parents' room and knocked.

"Come in." His mother was standing by the closet, brushing her dress. Her hair, which she had grown to her shoulders, was streaked with a pale gray. She looked up and smiled.

"They're here," Quentin said.

The bathroom door opened and his father stepped out, sideburns wet from shaving.

"They're here," Quentin said again.

"Sam, help me with my dress."

His father tugged at the zipper and fastened the clasp, his fingers working carefully, delicately.

"Hold still, Laura," he said. "Stop twitching."

"Knock-knock. Come in. Thank you." Scobie stood in the doorway, grinning. "Hello."

"Hello, darling."

Matthew, Susan, and Franny crowded in behind Scobie. "Hello, Quentin. How are you?"

"Fine."

Scobie stood back and looked him over. "Mother, this boy needs food."

"He won't eat any."

"Speaking of which, they're waiting for us downstairs," his father said.

"Yes," his mother said. "I thought we could eat a big meal now and then just have a snack tonight."

"Who's sleeping where?" Matthew asked.

"You and Scobie are with Quentin," she said. "The girls have their own room."

"I'll show you," Quentin said.

The corridor was patterned with shafts of sunlight, and, leading the way, Quentin felt as if he were walking into a camera, into the fluttering lens of a magic eye. Shadows lay at the end, modulated depths and shades broken only by gleaming doorknobs. His hands were heavy again, swinging at his sides—objects he seemed to be carrying.

"Here." He opened the door and stepped inside.

"Ah, yes," Scobie said, climbing over the mound of clothes cluttering the floor. "Quentin has settled in."

*   *   *

The room was silent except for the ticking of the alarm clock and an occasional boat whistle out on the canal. It was sunset. Through the window Laura could see a dull red brightening the sky. She rolled over and snapped on the bedside lamp. Sam was still asleep, his hands tucked under his pillow. She lit a cigarette and leaned back. A pile of gaily wrapped Christmas presents lay on a table in the corner. For a moment, she remembered the childhood joy of traveling from New York to Northfield, Massachusetts, where her great-aunt Judy had lived in a long white house, with stables at one end and a library at the other. In between were rooms and rooms—a living room with violet cushions and a grand piano, a dining room with a row of windows overlooking the apple orchard, a kitchen with a shiny brick floor and a fireplace big enough to stand in, and, upstairs, bedrooms with brass beds and finely painted porcelain washbasins. At Christmas, the whole family would gather, cousins driving from as far away as Cincinnati. The hallway would fill up with boots and overcoats, fires would be burning in all the fireplaces. A huge Christmas tree, cut just that week, would stand in a corner of the living room, and slowly the presents would accumulate under the fresh pine needles—ribbons and tinsel and gold paper all merging into one tantalizing glow. Judy's father and husband had both been ministers, and so there was always a trek to church across the snowy fields and hymn singing in the living room—with Judy, already in her seventies, banging on the piano—and a long grace before Christmas dinner. How she had loved that house, and how strange to find it, on a trip to Northfield to visit her father's grave just two years ago, belonging to a nearby boys' school—the beneficiary of Judy's will. Laura had walked through the rooms—the library a clubroom, the living room a center for black students, the bedrooms junior-faculty apartments—and wondered what had happened to all her Christmas playmates.

Outside, the fair had opened, and the lights and noises penetrated the quiet room.

Laura put out her cigarette. After Christmas, she decided, she would take Quentin shopping. The only clothes he seemed to have were hand-me-downs from Scobie and Matthew, and they were dirty and full of holes.

She looked at the clock. "Sam," she whispered. "Sam."

The black, open mouth swallowed a witch with blinking red eyes. Just below, on the same cardboard mural, a whore sang to the stars, her massive thighs stretched in pleasure. Sam slowly looked at the other paintings adorning the fun house. They were all oversized, grotesque, garish. Yet here and there he found evidence—a line, a shade—of artistry. The noise of gunshots and breaking plates filled the night. Hundreds of small childern, dressed impeccably in skirts and capes and caps, had been brought to the fair by their parents; the fathers had longish, carefully styled hair, and the mothers had faces etched with makeup. The Ferris wheel and the merry-go-round were the most beautiful Sam had ever seen: the seats carved and gilded and sumptuously covered with a soft red material that looked like velvet. Beyond the fair, the houses of Venice rose into darkness, a few lights on behind a few windows, the old walls faded and smoothed by centuries of rain and wind. Italy, he thought, would be a good place to live—if he could only find a house by the sea. And the thought of his imminent retirement suddenly took him from the fair and spun him back to his own saddened state: fifty-three, sagging in the middle, gray-haired, and tired of serving his country. He had things of his own to do. He wanted to paint again. For twenty years he had been rising at six and driving to an office in some embassy, greeting his secretary, drinking a second cup of coffee, straightening his tie, and walking down the ringing corridor to the nine-o'clock staff meeting. Twenty years! The waste involved—his knowledge, his experience, his time and his effort and his care. He would take it all with him when he retired. It would be useless. Except that it was his life, the sum total of twenty professional years. Nothing is ever wasted, he thought. Nothing. Ever.

"Hey, Dad, let's ride the bumper cars," Matthew said, pulling him by the arm.

Sam and Quentin in one car, Matthew and Scobie in another, they sped around the circular inclined raceway. There were about fifteen other cars on the track, with a major collision every few seconds. Sam's knees did not quite fit under the miniature dashboard, his glasses kept slipping down his nose, and his checked tweed cap threatened to fly off in his wake. Laura and Susan and Franny stood on the edge of the raceway and laughed hysterically. Quentin, sitting next to him, had his knees up under his chin and his hands clutching the dashboard, and his long hair flew out behind him like a frazzled weather net.

And yet, Sam thought, taking his car around a corner

and sending Matthew and Scobie into a spin, I am not so badly off, not really. Three healthy sons. A beautiful wife. In Venice for Christmas. And not so paunchy. Not so tired.

"Dad, look out!" Quentin screamed.

Hit broadside by a grinning Matthew, Sam's car twisted a full circle and smashed into the rubber guardrail. He backed the car around and took chase.

And not so slow, either.

After lunch the next day, Scobie and Susan took a boat out to the Lido. The sky was overcast, the water dark green. Small whitecaps nudged the buoys. Scobie and Susan sat near the bow, holding hands. The Venetian houses faded behind them, and before them the newer, French-looking buildings of the Lido grew in size. It was cold and damp. Scobie tightened his scarf around his neck and turned up the fur collar of his coat. The wind made his eyes water. The smell—sea, brine—was almost mythological, he thought. A smell designed for stone, sirens, stars. In Greece, where he had spent four years as a child, the smell had been the same, only warmed by the sun filtering through the closed shutters of his bedroom window every morning and wakening him with a longing for adventure. That sensation— the hot laziness, the lapping waves below the terrace, the cool shadows of the rooms—had been with him ever since, a romantic contact with the earth. The landscape itself had seemed touched by a kind of longing, an almost religious melancholy. Objects stood out with special clarity. Sounds carried with special vibrancy. From Greece, he supposed, came his love for beauty of surface, tone, shade, melody, abstraction in the simplest sense: a pale wall in a patch of sunlight, a curtain dancing with dust, a woman's fingers idly twisting the stem of a glass. He was constrained by his senses. And his senses constantly led him away from his own time, his own place.

"What's the matter?" Susan asked.

"Nothing."

"Yes, there is. What's wrong?"

Susan's white, angular face, surrounded by a scarf, smiled at him. Her eyes were large and blue, her fine lips settled, resolute. He leaned over and kissed her.

"Do you realize this is our first Christmas together in eight years?" he said. "The family's, I mean."

"Christmas is always disappointing," she said.

"I guess."

The boat swung to starboard and rubbed in against the dock. Scobie and Susan followed a large group of laughing teen-agers onto the pavement and down a wide boulevard.

After Venice, the Lido looked dismal in the gray afternoon light. They walked under the bare elm trees, past pink villas that had been converted into summer hotels, until they reached the beach. There they turned, the sand and striped cabanas at their left, the trees and hedges of a park at their right. There were only a few people out walking. On the beach a man and a boy were trying to fly a kite. Seagulls circled the long, rolling waves, now and then dipping down for fish. Their cawing—orchestrated, precise—reminded Scobie of his English boarding school, the Saturday afternoons he used to spend walking along the crumbling shale cliffs, listening to the gulls and watching

the trawlers move slowly up and down the Bristol Chan-
nel. There the grayness had been a drizzle, and the gulls
had called to him from a sky as thick as clouds. Everything
remained intact in his head. He never forgot: the cold
mornings, the long, wooden eating tables, the underheated
classrooms, the headmaster's daughter, the hitchhike to
London, his drunken, rainy rages along the country lanes
shaking with lightning. These remained, though the true
misery of being there, his pointless anger, had mellowed,
so that now, while he remembered he had hated that
school, he could hate it no longer. Time had passed, and
with it accuracy. Memory had become poetic: it is spring,
and suddenly, after months of rain and mist, the sun sets
fire to the hidden, fertile seeds and the whole world opens
up like a bud; the fields turn bright green; the hillsides
sparkle with flowers; the rocks are covered with a soft, un-
ending moss; hundreds of birds flutter and sing in the
ivy; and he sits in the small, grassy graveyard of the church,
alone, a bottle of wine by his feet, smoking a cigarette,
listening, smelling, and then, his head casting a shadow
across his lap, reading—reading in a way he would never
be able to read again, as if these words, these magical
sentences, were as real as the countryside around him.

Susan took him by the arm and turned him around so
that he stood facing the stolid stone façade, the gravel paths
and clipped hedges and boarded-up windows, of the Hôtel
des Bains.

Wandering from room to room of the Doges' Palace, his
neck strained from staring up at Tintorettos, Matthew
marveled that here, in perhaps the most beautiful city in

the world, he found not purity and light but darkness and fear. Every stone had been lifted by hands commanded to lift. Every painting had been commissioned to awe an ambassador. Every sculpture, every tapestry was there only because someone, somewhere, had wanted more power or money or prestige. The architecture was graceful, yes—the fine Gothic arches elegant in their quiet rows. But inside he saw only immodest greed. The strong had done what they could; the weak had done what they had to do. So Venice was built. Even today he saw nothing but things. Beautiful things. Shirts, ties, shoes, gloves, books, food, liquor, pens, china, perfume. Too much, too beautiful— this palace running on and on, rooms growing larger, the brilliant polished floors and the glutted, swirling frescoes and the gold ceilings and the tarnished mirrors. And to think that all through his childhood he had thought the Bridge of Sighs was a lovers' bridge, some splendid marble pathway to bliss. Now here it was, a short walk across space to prison.

Franny whispered, "I hate this place."

One by one, the dungeons passed. Clean. Swept. But once, right here, the scene of death. He shivered.

They returned to the palace and walked down stairways and empty corridors, trying to find their way out. Franny's cheeks were red from the cold. Her hiking boots clunked on the marble floors. Matthew pulled his wool cap down over his ears and took her hand.

He and Scobie used to hold hands, he remembered—a habit they had picked up in Greece. But once back in the States they had stopped. It was too sissy. Too frightening, he suspected, such intimacy. Later, when they were in

Rome, they had seen other children their age holding hands, but they never did it again themselves. They were already self-conscious. Their love took other, more hidden forms: the comfort of shared memories, and a strange, mutual protection—keeping up, looking after, sheltering.

Franny pushed open a heavy door and they stepped out into a courtyard.

"The sun!" she cried. "Look, Matthew."

Above them the clouds had pulled apart enough to let through a long arc of golden light.

The sun is Greece, he thought. Columns like prayer lifted toward the sky. The dry earth. The water cool and green above the rocks. The pines. The boats pulled up for the night. The fishnets spread to dry. And always the sun—hot and clear, or streaked (dawn, dusk), or just a hint of violet in the mountains. Always there, warming everything. How he loved Greece, and how he missed his little apartment, the stove, the view of the Acropolis, the bakery, the market, the tiny glasses of ouzo, the olives.

"Are Scobie and Susan going back to Greece after Christmas?" Franny asked.

"I don't think so. They'll keep traveling, I suppose."

"Matthew?"

"Yes?"

"What are we going to do?"

"Go back, of course."

"No, I mean after that."

"I don't know."

"Do you want to stay in Greece forever?"

"I don't know. Maybe."

"I think I want to go back to school," she said.

And here, Matthew thought, the problem presents itself: what to do? Stay in Greece or go back to America? In Greece, he had clarity, quiet, time, memories. He studied the language, read, wrote. In America, he had nothing except a vague connection to the land. It was unhealthy, he suspected, to live at the center of the world. Once in America, only America exists. Everything seems of equal importance, therefore everything is equally unimportant. So signs and mysteries abound, hints and clues. Americans are all amateur detectives. They read the clouds, the papers, the songs for spiritual information, then shrivel up with what they think they have learned. Sleep badly. Take pills. Worry. Even his friends worried. Even he worried. But all those mountains and rivers, the deserts and the snow, the ghosts of buffalo and the threats of holocaust. Perhaps—this bothered him—Greece had been something like that in her heyday. Perhaps the peace he felt there now was the peace of powerlessness. Problems had assumed human proportions again. People laughed and shrugged. They cared but they didn't worry. The sea and the marble and the pines calmed the spirit. Or killed it— laid it in the eager hands of waiting colonels. The stubborn antiquity of Greece sometimes struck him as a manufactured dream, a distant product of the American imagination. Perhaps, after all, he must live in the middle of the machine, down among the bits and pieces of broken technology, down where truth was a mindless computation.

"Well," he said, "I can't go on tutoring English the rest of my life, so I'll probably want to go back to the States. At least for a while. See what happens."

"We could always come back."

"That's right." He blew into his cold hands. "Anyway, I miss my friends sometimes. Even if they are crazy."

"God, I'd like to hear some good music," she said.

He laughed. "It wouldn't be so bad. For a while."

Quentin was a victim of genetic structures, biological arrangements. He was bone and flesh. A collection of particulars: eyes, ears, nose, mouth. These were the basics, the instruments of truth. What he saw, heard, smelled, tasted, he knew. He trusted the evidence, the impulses, his heart. For him there was no other way. He understood nothing. His father, his brothers—they understood. They comprehend the game. "Play or perish," Scobie said. "You're either on the top or on the bottom," Matthew said. "Man lives by his commitments," his father said. "Without involvement, we are nothing," his mother said. And they were right, absolutely correct. They knew enough to stand firm. Quentin drifted. His brain was cloudy. He seldom moved, his muscles sagged, his back stooped. But why? *Why?*

Cleaning his glasses, which were held together with paper clips, Quentin leaned forward and peered at the painting: mother and child. And another woman, a stranger. Bellini.

He stood back for a clearer view, thinking, The sad faces cause great grief to the background. The darkness is luminescent, like black tears. Only the child is calm. He senses his mother's hands and is calm.

Quentin continued along the wall of paintings, wondering what in the world had made these men paint so beautifully. But as he looked he began to understand that each stroke of color, each aspect of composition was tied to a childhood vision of single objects surrounded by mystery. The backgrounds were either blurred or fantastically detailed. He slowly warmed to these ancient gentlemen with their intricate memories. He felt with them a sudden kinship—they could have discussed the complex working of love and the frightening colors hiding in the sky. They could have been friends.

Quentin left the museum, passed the British consulate, crossed a bridge, and walked into a maze of alleyways. The sun was setting. Pink light touched the old walls. The wind was intensified by the narrow streets. He shrugged down into his coat and walked quickly.

Soon, he thought, he must learn how to fight his way free of this weight, or he would become a giddy, guilty nothing. The world conspires to reduce us all to such helplessness, Quentin thought, reminded of George, his eleventh-grade roommate, baffled and broken by fear and destroyed by his own hand simply because a thick-brained headmaster had said he was going to tell his father he smoked dope. Period. End of a life. End of a consciousness. So what was there to fight back with, Quentin wondered. Commitment to a circle, involvement with a spiral —this was madness.

He passed a wall, a garden, a fountain, a square. He saw people bustling with Christmas cheer. He saw green scarves and shiny shoes and laughing children. He saw stores filled with presents. He saw the colorful, steamy windows of restaurants. He saw a sky turning red with sunset.

*   *   *

There is no getting at the truth of things, Laura thought in the dining room of the Danieli, looking at her sons, her husband, Susan and Franny, the gleaming silverware, the candles, the black-coated headwaiter taking orders in his little pad. There is no understanding the way the heart works. She did her best, she tried to understand, but she knew each effort was itself only a manifestation of love. Ever since she was a girl growing up in New York City—and she remembered suddenly, with great pleasure, the Christmas trees on Park Avenue and the smell of roasting chestnuts along Forty-second Street and the bright shop-windows along Fifth—ever since she was a little girl, she had been trying to understand what it was that made people demand so much of themselves. She realized that working could be a kind of fulfillment. She realized that forti-tude could define reality, create security. She understood that. But what made people place themselves in a posi-tion where they could be happy only in comparison with other people? It was all connected with the way the heart works, she suspected. But it was muddled, and she could not see the connection. She saw one kind of love here, and another kind of love there. What happened in be-tween? How did so many people get stuck between child-hood love, which was innocent if anything was, and grown-up love, which, for the most part, was only false knowl-edge?

"I would like to propose a toast," Scobie said, lifting his glass of wine. "To Mom and Dad."

"To Mom and Dad."

"Hear, hear."

"Thank you."

"And also," Scobie continued, grinning around the table, "to the spirit of Christmas."

"To the spirit of Christmas."

"Yes, to spirit."

"In general," Scobie said. "To spirit."

"Good toast."

"Thank you."

"And I," Sam said, holding his glass aloft, "would like to offer a toast *specifically* to your mother, whose idea it was, you will remember, to bring us all together in Venice for Christmas."

"To Ma."

"Good cheer."

"I'll drink to that."

"And I," Quentin said, "would like to drink to Mom and Dad's uncertain future."

"May it be bright."

"Good luck."

"God bless."

"What *are* you going to do?" Scobie demanded.

"Who knows, dear?"

"Live on a boat," Sam said.

"No."

"Sell everything we own and live on a boat."

"No, I want a nest."

"Where, Mother?"

"In America."

"Oh, Mom, you don't want to live in America," Matthew said. "What would you do? You don't know anybody there."

"You mother wants to participate," Sam said.

"In what?"

"America."

"I'm tired of traveling," she said.

Dinner arrived. Veal, mushrooms, artichokes, shrimp, salad. The table was covered with food. Three waiters served from a small side tray. The candle flames bent, sputtered, straightened. Her children, faces flushed, sat around her and exchanged toasts and laughed. Wonder, disbelief—that is what she felt. At this very moment—no, tomorrow; or was it yesterday?—her brother, Paul, and his family were sitting at their table in Wilmington, Delaware, eating *their* Christmas dinner. She could imagine clearly his heavy, Irish face bent studiously above the steaming turkey, Joan's panicky warnings and advice, their children's amused praise. So different, the lives they led. Paul in Wilmington for twenty years, she moving from home to home, country to country, each embassy merging into the next, each new group of friends gradually dimming into one strange world of vague relationships. The only thing she and Paul had in common now was their childhood, their strain of weak Irish sadness. Whenever they met— every two or three years—they wept, Paul drinking martinis until his one bad eye grew glassy and rolled up in what seemed either a grimace of madness or a silent howl of love. Together, they would sit and talk about their sep- arate lives and children until, inevitably, they were back in New York or Northfield, children themselves, and then Paul would quietly put down his glass, kiss her good night, and slowly, almost delicately, climb the stairs to bed.

The restaurant chimed with their talk. They were the only ones there. Everyone else was home for Christmas Eve. She worried that the waiters and cooks might have their Christmas spoiled by her lingering family.

Would Scobie and Susan *ever* get married?

Quentin needed new clothes and a winter coat, and, really, a haircut—a trim.

Matthew was glowing! Beaming!

"Scobie," she asked, "who said, 'Only the moments exist, but not their imaginary combination'?"

" '. . . just as a man has no life; not even one of his nights exists; each moment we live exists, but not their imaginary combination.' Borges. 'A New Refutation of Time.' Ah, Mother, Mother—Merry Christmas." He lifted his glass.

"Merry Christmas, darling," she said.

At eleven-thirty they left the Danieli and walked to St. Mark's. It was a clear, cold night. The water of the Grand Canal was still, shimmering with starlight. Sam buttoned the collar of his overcoat and sank his hands deep into his pockets. He felt light-headed from the wine. His stomach growled. Laura took his arm and touched her cheek to his shoulder. Scobie, Susan, Matthew, Franny, and Quentin walked ahead in a long line, arms linked. Their words and laughter reached him in fragments. He noticed that Quentin was as tall as Scobie. Matthew was the shortest. They all walked with the same rolling shuffle —a sailor's walk, he thought, and wondered if he walked the same way. Far out on the water a boat whistle hooted.

The square was empty. All the expensive stores under the arcade were closed. Here and there light shone through the windows of a café. The stones of the square glistened. The cathedral was dark, but next to it, two stories high, was a bright Christmas tree.

"There's no midnight Mass," Laura said, squinting at a bulletin posted on the cathedral doors.

Scobie stared over her shoulder. "How can there be no midnight Mass on Christmas Eve?"

"Well, there isn't."

"The man at the *pensione* told me about another church back by the restaurant," Franny said. "San Zaccaria."

"O.K. About-face."

They turned and made their way back past the Doges' Palace and along the Grand Canal.

Sometimes Sam worried that he had brought his sons up so freely they would never be able to function in a world of shifting freedoms. They got along, they managed, but they seemed to have difficulty attaching themselves to anything that might lead to a career. Doctors? Lawyers? Diplomats? No—they laughed at the idea, as if it were a joke. Yet there was a drive in them, a muted ambition, that made them *want* to attach themselves. He was sure of that. But the old tasks had lost their value. They felt they would be implicated in crime if they were to work for criminals. And they saw everybody as a criminal. They trusted no one: they traced events back to their beginnings and discovered only deceit. True, deceit abounds. Evil abounds. Crime abounds. But you've got to live. You've got to take your stand and say, "Here I'll fight." You do your best. You tread mills. You die anonymously. But what else is there? You pick a generality with which you generally agree and make it your cause. That's it. That's all there is. What would they do with their drive—their talent, for Godsake? They *were* talented, his sons. They had a mission: to help; to counsel; to stand with others like them and do their best to hold men back from the brink.

"Look, there." Quentin pointed. "Follow the crowd."

They turned left and entered a dark, narrow street that twisted along for about fifty yards and then opened into a small square. Sam could hear a fountain dripping near-by. To his right rose the church.

" 'San Zaccaria,' " Matthew read.

Inside, the church was crowded with midnight wor-shipers. The service had not started. Dozens of candles quivered before the altar. An organ was playing. There were four dark wooden confessional booths on both sides of the church, with people waiting in line at each one.

"We'll have to split up," Scobie whispered.

Sam found two seats at the back and sat down with Laura.

The organ continued to play a deep, rumbling hymn, and, from an obscured balcony high above the nave, a choir started singing.

Sam looked sideways at the nearest confessional booth. It was open in the front, with a drawn curtain hiding the priest's face and chest. There were small, screened win-dows on either side of the booth, through which two kneel-ing confessors appeared to speak simultaneously. The priest's hands lay on the curled wooden molding of the booth's entrance. Clasping and unclasping, touching each other and settling again, they looked like the quivering candles. They were beautiful old hands, pale and strong and veined. Their fluttering seemed the movement of anxiety; they seemed to be absorbing the pain of the secret words whispered through the windows.

When Scobie and Matthew and Quentin were children and they lived in Virginia, Sam had had to drive the family north to Long Island every Christmas to spend the week with his parents. He remembered arriving late at night, the country roads slick with ice, pulling into his parents' driveway and parking the car under the tree that his mother always decorated with blue lights. The boys, who had been sleeping in the back seat, would jump up with excitement and clamber from the car into his mother's arms. There would be a large Christmas tree in the front hall and a fire in the fireplace, and his mother and father, who had fallen asleep waiting for them, would look dazed and happy as the suitcases and presents were carried in. The next day, the boys would go sledding—screaming and laughing and rolling in the snow, piled three high on the old sled. Christmas Eve his mother would read them *'Twas the Night Before Christmas* and then they would go to bed, while he and Laura and his parents stayed up, putting presents under the tree and talking. On Christmas day, Ken and Nancy and their children would drive over and the family would, as his mother said every year, "Spend Christmas properly. Together." In a way, Sam missed those days, though at the time they had often been painful. Returning home is always the same. Memories push in from the walls; the smells rise up like ghosts; everything you touch—the plates, the photograph albums, the books—is haunted by your own childhood. But the boys had loved it, and that was the part Sam missed. They had been ecstatic with the mystery of the snow and the trees and the bay gleaming out beyond the lawn.

The service began.

Lying in bed, his hands behind his head, Scobie stared through the window at the clear Venetian sky and listened to the heavy breathing of his sleeping brothers. The room was bright with the morning sun.

"Get up," he said.

Matthew and Quentin didn't hear him, or ignored him. They were buried beneath their blankets.

He rubbed his feet along the warm sheets. The walls of the room were covered with small, dancing circles of light. He could smell coffee being brewed down in the kitchen.

"Get up," he said, louder. "Rise and shine."

His brothers didn't move.

"Hey, it's Christmas."

Matthew's fingers pulled back his blanket. His eyes opened.

"Good morning," Scobie said.

"Good morning," Matthew said, smiling.

Scobie ran into the bathroom and turned on the shower. Matthew listened to the water drumming against the plastic curtain and Scobie's sputtering, whispered singing. Through the window he could see a square of pale-blue sky. He stretched and yawned.

"Quentin. Time to get up."

"No." Quentin's voice was muffled under his blankets.

"It's Christmas."

"I don't care."

"Get up."

"I'm too tired."

Matthew continued to watch the sky through the window. A wisp of cloud appeared and was slowly blown away.

"Shave, shave, I love to shave," Scobie was muttering in the bathroom. "Wonderful shave, beautiful shave—"

"Shut up!" Quentin shouted.

The bathroom door opened. Scobie's lathered face peered around at Quentin. "What's this?"

"Stop it."

"What?"

"That noise."

"I'm singing, for Godsake. Where's your Christmas cheer?" The door shut.

Matthew stretched again and sat up on the edge of his bed. The floor was cold. He looked over at his brother's bed. Quentin had rolled back his blankets and was staring at the ceiling.

"Good morning."

"Good morning."

"Are you getting up?"

"I'm thinking about it." Quentin watched Matthew stand and skip across the floor to the bathroom. The shower water hummed again. Scobie came out and started dressing. His hair was wet and brushed straight back from his forehead. He whistled as he pulled on his jeans and unfolded a clean shirt. Over his shoulder, a seagull slowly circled in the sky. Quentin threw back his covers and rose.

"Why Quentin, have you considered this carefully?" Scobie said.

"I always get up early," Quentin replied, standing. "To do my exercises."

He opened the bathroom door. Matthew was combing his hair before the steamy mirror. Quentin stepped under the hot water and showered, then dried himself with a large pink towel. When he returned to the bedroom, Matthew was sitting on his bed, tying his shoes.

"Where's Scobie?"

"He's gone down for breakfast," Matthew said.

Quentin dressed hurriedly—paint-stained black pants, heavy Army boots, a flannel shirt, and a corduroy vest a friend had given him in college. Then he brushed his hair and tied it back in a ponytail.

"Ready?" Matthew asked. He was standing by the door.

"Yeah."

Together, they walked down the stairs to the dining room. Sunlight hung in the windows like mirrors. Quentin's eyes felt as if he needed new glasses. He followed Matthew through the glass door into the dining room. His shirt kept bunching up beneath his vest.

"Good morning," Laura said.

"Good morning."

She looked around the table at her sons, at Sam, Susan, and Franny, all bent over their coffee and rolls, then out at the water and the sky and the seagulls and the sun on the stone.

"Well, Mother," Scobie said. "We did it."

"What's that, darling?"

"We're together for Christmas. First time in eight years."

"Is that what it's been?" Sam asked. "I was trying to figure it out last night."

"Eight years," Scobie said. "I was a sophomore in high school."

"That's a long time."

"Yes, it is," she said. "That's why I want a nest."

"I understand, Mother," Quentin said.

"I know you do. But your father keeps saying he wants to live on a boat."

"I just don't want to sit down and die somewhere," Sam said.

"I understand that," Matthew said.

Through the window Sam saw a large tanker sliding out to sea.

"Dad, when do you actually stop working?" Matthew asked.

"This spring."

"Has everyone finished his coffee?" Laura asked. "Shall we go upstairs and open our presents?"

"By all means," Scobie said, pushing back his chair and standing. "Mother, lead on."

Sam swallowed a last mouthful of coffee and, his old Abercrombie shoes creaking on the carpet, followed his family up the stairs, aware that, in a way, he and Laura had reached the end of a journey, that his sons, once only cells of light in her body, this morning rose before him as dominant as his parents.

Laura opened the bedroom door and stood blinking in

the bright light. It's all a matter of balancing between the temptation to remember and the sympathetic magic of this still moment, she thought: the sunlit room, the presents piled on the table, the tray of small Campari bottles sitting by the window—this single quivering instant of love.

She handed Sam a present in gold paper.

Sam propped his cigarette in an ashtray and held the small box cautiously, as though it were a bird.

Scobie sipped his Campari and grinned out the window.

Matthew touched Franny's hand.

Quentin, blushing, clinked glasses with Susan and turned to watch his father.

Below, on the Grand Canal, a long white ocean liner gracefully circled the harbor, once, to give the tourists a view of Venice.